The Wrong Coat

A Fishen-Rodd Mystery

Suzanne Young
March, 2018

Sybown Press

Cover Designer: Karen Phillips

Sybown Press
9028 West 50th Lane, #1
Arvada, CO 80002-4441

This book is dedicated
to all you readers.

Other books by Suzanne Young

The Edna Davies Mystery series:
Murder by Yew, 2009
Murder by Proxy, 2011
Murder by Mishap, 2012
Murder by Christmas, 2013
Murder by Arrangement, 2015
Murder by Decay, 2016

Chapter 1

"This isn't my coat." Beryl Fishen pushed the garment toward the young attendant.

"I'm sorry, ma'am, but this is the one you described." The teenager looked concerned but determined. "Full-length, black coat with silver buttons."

"Well," huffed Beryl, annoyed at the carelessness of youths in general. "I'm sorry too, but you've given me the wrong coat."

"It certainly looks like your coat, Beryl." Nadine Rodd tugged gently on her friend's arm, pulling her out of line. Theater-goers behind Beryl were anxious to find their own coats and leave the tiny lobby of the local playhouse. "How do you know it's not your coat?"

"Take a look at that collar." Beryl waved the offending article toward Nadine.

"I see." She recoiled. "You're right. Looks like pancake makeup. What's the saying from the old ad … 'ring around the collar'?"

"Not only that," Beryl continued as if her point had not already been made, "there's no mad money."

"Mad money?"

"Here," Beryl turned the facing around to display a square piece of silver silk with black lettering. "No safety pin."

Nadine shrugged. "Doesn't need one. It's a perfectly good label, despite the age of the coat."

Ignoring the observation, Beryl explained. "I fasten a ten behind the label in case of an emergency. You know, like if some young hoodlum was to grab my purse."

"*Were* to grab your purse," Nadine corrected.

"What?"

"If some young hoodlum *were* to grab your purse," Nadine repeated. She taught high school English and composition for 45 years before retiring three years ago. "It's hypothetical, supposition, so you should use the subjunctive."

Beryl shook her head as she plunged a hand into one of the coat's side pockets. "I lost my coat, ten dollars and my house key and all you do is stand there giving me grammar lessons. Who cares how hoodlums steal my purse?" She pulled several crumpled papers from the pocket. "Here, see if there's a name or address on any of those," she said, shoving the wad into Nadine's hand.

While Beryl searched the other side pocket, Nadine straightened the papers, finding a fast-foods receipt, a crumpled grocery list and three foil candy wrappers among the lot. Smoothing a piece of paper slightly larger than the rest, she studied it, front and back. After a long moment, she frowned and held up the slip to Beryl. "What do you make of this?"

Halted in her search, Beryl lowered her reading glasses from atop a mass of soft white curls in order to study the sheet. "It's a library receipt for four books that were due yesterday." Conceding to the superior knowledge of her literary friend, she brightened. "Think we can track the thief through her library card?"

Nadine shook her head in answer and glanced around as if expecting to catch someone lurking nearby. "Turn it over," she whispered.

Beryl flipped the paper and read aloud the three words scrawled on the back. "Help. Murder. Frame."

"Shhh," Nadine stage-whispered. "Not so loud."

"Doesn't seem like a particularly big secret," Beryl said without lowering her voice. Holding the printed side toward her friend, she grunted. "These titles sound like mysteries to me. It's only a guess, mind you, but I would say the reader wants help in looking for stories about persons framed for murder."

Undaunted by Beryl's sarcastic tone, Nadine still spoke quietly. "But look how shaky the writing is on the back. I think whoever wrote those words was frightened."

"Or elderly," Beryl responded. "Or maybe she has palsy."

Nadine wasn't giving up. She showed Beryl the grocery list. "This handwriting isn't shaky," she observed in a triumphant tone.

"It also looks like someone else wrote it," Beryl retorted. "Nothing strange about that. I'm guessing my kleptomaniac doesn't live alone. Obviously, it was a different person that scribbled on the library receipt."

"*Who* scribbled," Nadine said quietly. "A person is a *who* not a *that*."

Scowling at her friend, Beryl took the scraps of

paper from Nadine. Stuffing everything back into the coat pocket, she turned to glower at the young usher. The teen, busy assisting some of the more elderly patrons to locate their overcoats, seemed unaware of the daggers being thrown her way.

Oblivious to the silent scolding she'd also received from those piercing brown eyes, Nadine put out a hand to stop Beryl. "Let's wait here. We're in no hurry and there are only a few coats left. None of them look even remotely like the one you're holding, so whoever has your coat already left. Maybe she'll realize her mistake and return before we leave.

Although impatient and slightly irritated, Beryl knew Nadine was right, so the two women stood aside and waited until they were the only patrons in the lobby and both portable chrome racks held nothing but a disarray of wire hangers. Finally, Beryl started toward the young woman who, with a fleeting glance in her direction, spun around and disappeared beyond a door marked "Employees Only." Moments later, she reemerged with a tall, dark-haired woman who looked to be in her mid-forties. They'd never met, but Beryl knew her from advertising flyers and newspaper ads as Tish Nanquette, the theater manager.

"Good evening, ladies." The woman nodded in greeting. "Ashley tells me you think you have the wrong coat."

"I don't just *think*, I *know* this is not my coat." Annoyed by the manager's cynical look and tone, Beryl proceeded to explain about the stained collar and about the mad money she kept pinned behind the designer's label. "What's more," she concluded, "my house key is in the pocket of my coat." She didn't explain further but let the woman assume Beryl would be locked out of her house.

"I'm sure you understand that we're a small playhouse staffed mostly with volunteers." Tish's voice was soft and soothing as she apparently chose to ignore Beryl's pending predicament. "We depend on our patrons to manage their own coats. Ashley stays in the lobby as a courtesy, to assist where needed." Her expression turned suitably apologetic as she continued. "You know, most theaters don't even provide a place for coats. We offer these racks and hangers as a convenience to you." The look she bestowed on the two elderly patrons was both conciliatory and pleased as she paused.

Beryl was beginning to think the woman was waiting for some sort of applause for her generosity when Tish continued, "I see that another of our evening's attendees has the same good taste as you." She beamed first at Beryl, then at Nadine as if she'd just settled everything to everyone's satisfaction. "When that person realizes there's been a mix-up, most assuredly, she'll be back." Mrs. Nanquette nodded as if cueing the senior citizens to agree.

Said seniors only stared until Tish plucked a program from the table and, pulling a pen from her skirt pocket, she circled the theater's phone number. "Here," she said, handing the pamphlet to Beryl, "why don't you check back with us tomorrow? I'm sure we'll have heard something by then."

Beryl accepted the playbill and motioned for the pen. Writing in the top margin, she handed both back to the woman. "Here's my name and number," she said. "Perhaps you'll be good enough to call me. That seems more sensible, don't you think … for you to call me when my coat turns up, instead of my continuously phoning you to find out it hasn't?" She pursed her lips into a semblance of a smile for Tish's benefit before turning to Nadine. "Shall we go?" With that, the two friends went out into the late-September evening. Although the day had been warm, the Colorado night was chilly, so Beryl grudgingly donned the soiled garment.

"What are the odds of two coats being exactly alike in one very small community playhouse?" Nadine mused as, arm-in-arm, they headed down a dark residential side road toward Beryl's car.

"Not *exactly*," Beryl retorted. "Mine is new … and clean. I bought it at the factory outlet sale last week," Beryl said. "Since they aren't precisely one-of-a-kind designer items, I suppose it's not completely unreasonable that two black coats might look similar in dim light. You'd think, though, that people would make certain they have the right coat before running off."

Actually, Beryl was thinking it wasn't so much a big deal as it was unpleasant and inconvenient. Ten dollars wasn't much to lose, and besides the garage-door remote in her car, she had another house key hidden in the planter by the front door; but annoyance and inconvenience was giving her a headache and making her feel uncommonly petulant. She wanted her own coat back.

Chapter 2

The ladies appeared an odd couple as they walked slowly away from the small theater. At age 78, Beryl was still tall and stately. Having reached five feet, eight inches by age twelve, she'd been scolded by her mother to stand straight and be proud of her height, even if she did tower head and shoulders over her classmates for three or four of her most agonizing and impressionable teenage years. Six inches shorter and four years younger, Nadine was plump and walked slightly bent as if forever fighting a strong wind.

Approaching her 20-year-old Buick Lesabre, Beryl pulled the car keys from her purse and released the door locks with the remote. "Roll down the window," she ordered Nadine when they were both seated and the engine was on. "There's a peculiar odor coming from this coat, like wet wool or something. I don't want it stinking up my car."

In the enclosed space, Nadine, too, detected the scent and, although cold and shivering in her cotton jacket, she did as she was told. Sunnydale Senior Resort was little more than a ten-minute drive away, and she didn't know Beryl well enough to argue, particularly given her present mood.

"Why do you keep your house key in your coat

pocket instead of with the car key?" Nadine nodded at the ring dangling from the ignition as she settled back in her seat.

Beryl paused a moment, gathering her thoughts while she felt the familiar pang that always accompanied memories of her long-dead husband. "One of Michael's first burglary cases as a detective," she said with a brief glance at the side mirror before pulling away from the curb, "involved one of those quickie oil-change services where people wait for their cars. To make a long story short, one of the mechanics would take the key ring, hustle over to the address on the work sheet and go through the house, stealing whatever money or jewelry he could find. The oil change wouldn't be completed, of course, until the thief returned." Stopping at a red light, she looked at Nadine. "Ever since Michael explained the scheme to me, I've kept only the car key on my ring."

"What about the garage door remote?" Nadine was sure she'd discovered a flaw in Beryl's logic.

"Stick it in my purse whenever I leave the car with anyone."

"Oh, my," Nadine exclaimed. "I'd never think of that. Clever of those burglars, but very wicked." As Beryl eased through the intersection when the traffic light turned green, Nadine said, "That's right, your husband was a policeman, wasn't he."

The comment sounded like a statement rather than a question, so Beryl made no reply. The women were still getting to know each other, having met only two months earlier in the main building's beauty salon, shortly after Nadine moved into the housing complex. When, a week later, she and Beryl sat together in the van on a Sunnydale-sponsored trip to the Denver Botanic Gardens, their friendship began. Both being patrons of the arts, they found mutual interests and similar tastes in the local plays, concerts and movies.

"How is Hazel?" Nadine asked after several minutes had passed. She'd never met Beryl's next-door neighbor, but felt the need to break the growing silence. "As I remember, she lost her husband not too long ago. Is she coping?"

Beryl frowned, keeping her eyes on the road. "I'm not sure. Her daughter-in-law and granddaughter have been staying with her ever since George's funeral, so I've been keeping away … you know, letting them all have time to grieve. But earlier this week, I learned that Hazel's been bedridden for practically the entire time. As soon as I heard, I went over to see if I could help out in any way." She took a quick look at Nadine and rushed on. "I was shocked to see her."

"Why?" Nadine's question was urgent, responding to the astonishment in Beryl's statement.

"She was lying in bed." When that didn't raise an objection from her passenger, Beryl explained, "at ten-thirty in the morning. The curtains were drawn, making the room so dark I could have been mistaken, but she didn't look well at all." Almost to herself, Beryl said, "I wish I could have seen her eyes."

"Her eyes?" Nadine asked, her brow creased in confusion.

"She had a washcloth covering them," Beryl said. She was staring at the pickup in front of them, but described the image in her head. "Doe … that's the daughter-in-law … Doe said Hazel had a migraine and claimed that the warm cloth on her eyes helped with the pain. I thought it was more than that. Hazel was restless, but not from any headache. When she heard my voice, she reached out to take my hand. I'm sure that's what she wanted to do, but Doe got in my way to adjust Hazel's pillow." Beryl threw another quick look at Nadine. "As I said, the room was very dark, but I felt that Hazel was agitated, like she wanted to tell me something."

"But she never did?" Nadine prompted when Beryl said nothing further.

"No, she never had a chance," Beryl said, distracted as she slowed the car when the truck in front of them braked for a right-hand turn. She frowned at Nadine before looking away and resuming speed. "Doe kept hovering around the bed, like she didn't want me to get close to Hazel. Honestly, you'd think I'd come to kill her mother-in-law instead of paying a sick call on a neighbor."

"Maybe she's like that with all Hazel's visitors," Nadine suggested. "Is she simply being overly protective?"

Beryl narrowed her eyes as if the thought hadn't occurred to her. "Don't know. I want to find out who else's been to see Hazel. Since I didn't realize she was so ill, I've only visited that once."

"How did you hear of her illness?" Nadine asked.

"Henry Slater," Beryl replied as she slid her eyes toward Nadine and chuckled. "Or, rather, Clara Fairchild. Henry certainly lives up to his reputation as a ladies' man."

"Oh?" Nadine made the single word sound as though the information meant nothing to her.

"I've been enjoying our gorgeous weather, sitting on my patio. I don't know why it didn't dawn on me sooner, but it suddenly struck me that Henry has been in and out of Hazel's house quite often. Last Sunday, Clara showed up, so I waylaid her and asked what was up. Just to get her goat, I hinted that I thought Henry was courting Hazel."

Nadine choked a laugh. "I bet that got a rouse out of her."

"She did get a bit red in the face," Beryl admitted before turning more serious. "To tell the truth, she might have been more angry than upset. Said I shouldn't be joking about someone who was so sick. That's when she told me Hazel had been stricken down with grief and Henry was only paying respects to his friend's widow."

"What do you think is wrong with Hazel? Besides a migraine, do you think there really is something wrong with her eyes?" Nadine said.

Beryl nodded, the lines in her forehead deepening. "That's the impression I got." She paused for a minute before recalling, "The day of George's funeral was cloudy, so I thought it was odd that she was wearing dark glasses. I thought it was sort of rude when she didn't even take them off to speak to the mourners who were paying condolences on her husband's passing." Beryl paused briefly before offering an explanation. "I supposed her eyes might have been swollen from crying and she didn't want people to see."

"I understand his death was unexpected," Nadine

said.

Again, Beryl nodded, keeping her eyes on the road ahead. "Yes, it was. Poor Hazel … losing George just about eight months after their son's fatal heart attack."

"I can't imagine," Nadine murmured. She half-turned in her seat to face Beryl. "Do you suppose that's why Doe is so protective of her mother-in-law? Being a recent widow herself, Doe might simply be over-reacting."

"Hard to say," Beryl replied hesitantly. "Their son Steven had a weak heart and was hospitalized three or four years ago, so his passing wasn't entirely unexpected. The one good thing resulting from his death seems to be that Doe and her daughter have come to visit his parents more often. George was an insulin-dependent diabetic and travel became increasingly difficult, so it was nice of Doe to make the effort. Whenever the daughter-in-law did visit, Hazel was happy to have some relief in giving George his shots. Doe taught her daughter how to administer the insulin, so Kelsey could help out, too. The two were such a help to the older Bennets, it's a shame they didn't live closer."

Beryl paused, reflecting on George's decline before admitting to Nadine, "I didn't think his condition was life-threatening." Beryl was quiet for another minute, then said. "I did hear that, in addition to being diabetic, George suffered from depression and anxiety. He was put on medication for the symptoms not long after Steven's funeral. I didn't say anything to Hazel at the time, but I wondered if the prescription drugs might cause more harm than good."

"You said when you went to see Hazel, she was acting like she wanted to tell you something." Nadine brought the conversation back to one of Beryl's first revelations. "Do you think she could be suffering from depression or anxiety, as well? Maybe she's on medication that's causing her to act as jittery as you've described?"

Beryl shook her head. "According to Doe, Hazel's condition is nothing more than 'recent widow syndrome.'"

"What's *that*?" Nadine demanded. "I've been a widow for nearly a year and never heard of such a thing."

"Doe worked as a registered nurse before she married Steven Bennet, so I guess she considers herself some sort of expert on illnesses or symptoms or whatever, particularly when her opinions seem to have some logic to them. Also," Beryl added, risking a quick look at Nadine, "as you just pointed out, she's a recent widow herself."

"I object to being pigeon-holed," Nadine complained. "So, what are the symptoms of this particular disorder that Doe has diagnosed?"

"She believes Hazel is insecure and frightened because her life's partner is no longer at her side. According to Doe, those feelings are manifesting themselves into paranoia and delusions."

"Is that how Doe herself feels?" Nadine asked with a hint of sarcasm.

Beryl shrugged. "I doubt it. She was married to Steven for only about three years. Before that, she was a working divorcee … *and* she has a daughter who lives with her. I guess that makes a difference, having family around, particularly someone who relies on you to be strong."

"You said the daughter is helping to care for Hazel, too. Have you asked her opinion of her grandmother's condition?" Nadine asked.

Beryl didn't answer until she'd changed lanes and made a left turn onto a residential street. "Kelsey. Technically, she's a *step*-granddaughter. She's there sometimes, but she's also away a lot. When she *is* in town, she seems to be in her own little world. I've waved a couple of times when I've seen her heading off in Hazel's car, but she ignores me. She was the same way at George Bennet's funeral. Not very friendly. Seems downright stuck-up, if you ask me."

Nadine frowned. "What does this *step*-granddaughter do?"

"Good question." Beryl snorted a laugh of ridicule. "Several months ago, Hazel told me that Kelsey has become an aspiring actress and flies to various cities, auditioning for parts. She doesn't seem to be getting much work, for all the traveling she does. I get the impression that she is too much of a novice for her ambitions and expectations. Apparently, her acting career amounts to winning the leading role in her junior and senior high school plays. She's been spoiled to the point that she believes she's star material." Beryl shrugged. "Another feeling I have is that Doe doesn't mind buying airline tickets, but won't pay for an apartment. Hazel thinks Doe's having trouble cutting the apron strings."

"Only child?" Nadine guessed.

Beryl nodded.

"How old is Kelsey?" Nadine wondered aloud.

"I think she just graduated last year, so she's probably eighteen … nineteen, at most." Concentrating on the next turn, Beryl was silent for a minute or two before returning to her previous worry. "I do think Hazel's suffering from something serious, and it's more than 'recent widow syndrome.'"

"If you think she's trying to tell you something, why don't you phone her?" Nadine suggested.

"I tried that." Without looking at her passenger, Beryl said in a high-pitched, robotic parody, "*The number you have reached is unavailable. Please hang up and try again.*" She barked an angry laugh, returning to her own voice. "I don't see how staying in that darkened room is any sort of cure for what Doe has described, but family is family, and I can't argue with her. If it was me, well …" Beryl faltered and fell silent.

If it were I automatically popped into Nadine's head, but she refrained from correcting her friend's grammar, deciding that discretion truly *was* the better part of valor at the moment as she considered her friend's short fuse and present level of frustration. She pressed her lips firmly together as Beryl pulled into the courtyard of their continuing care retirement community or "CCRC," as it was commonly called.

Sunnydale Senior Resort was an upscale complex for citizens aged 50 or older, offering a variety of dwellings and life-styles from patio homes to hospice. Nadine's condominium was in a six-story high-rise, which residents, some with tongue-in-cheek, referred to as the "Big House." Two-story wings on the north and south joined the main structure to create a U-shape that cupped a west-facing courtyard. The second floor of each wing consisted of community and activity rooms, administrative offices, clinics, hospice and assisted-living suites while the space on the ground floor was reserved for boutiques, salons and dining. In fact, much of the ground floor was like a miniature shopping mall.

From her balcony on the third floor of the main building, Nadine could see most of the courtyard and border gardens below. The view to her left included Beryl's backyard.

Residents who preferred a separate dwelling lived in compact bungalows that bordered the north, south and west perimeters of the property. Beryl's one-bedroom was in the far southwest corner of the development. She'd been one of the first residents to sign a contract when the site was under construction, 12 years previously.

The circular drive of the main building and parking spaces along each of the extensions were screened from the rest of the property by three- to four-foot privet hedges and shrubs. Because of this barrier, after dropping Nadine off at the main door, Beryl didn't spot the emergency vehicles until she pulled around and entered the narrow alleyway that led to her cottage. Moving partway onto the dirt shoulder to edge past a fire truck and an ambulance, she pulled into her tiny garage and hurried across the narrow strip of grass to the lawn next door.

Four people in navy blue uniforms were standing on the sidewalk. A well-toned, fit young woman broke away from the group when she spotted Beryl rushing toward them, and introduced herself as Jessica Westin with the fire department.

"What's happening here?" Beryl asked with a rising sense of panic. "Was there a fire? Is anyone hurt? How's Hazel?"

The pretty brunette, who appeared to be in her early thirties, was every inch as tall as Beryl. She shook her head, her expression grave. "No, ma'am. No fire. We were called out on a medical emergency." The young firefighter paused before adding hesitantly. "I assume you're asking about the woman who lives here." At Beryl's solemn nod, the woman went on. "I'm afraid the news isn't good."

Beryl immediately knew the meaning of those few words. Even if she hadn't been married to a policeman, she'd seen enough movies and watched enough television to understand that Hazel was dead. "Was it an accident? Where is her daughter-in-law? Her granddaughter? Is anyone with her?" Beryl realized she was babbling, but she couldn't help herself. She had no idea that her neighbor had been so ill. The shocking news didn't make sense.

"I have no answers for you at this time, ma'am," Jessica said, taking Beryl gently by the arm and leading her back toward her own small bungalow. "Were you good friends? Would you like me to call someone to stay with you?" When Beryl shook her head, unable to speak, the young firefighter went on in a soft, soothing voice. "I'll tell the family you were asking for her. It's late, so I don't think they'll call you before morning."

"I wonder if Doe will bother," Beryl muttered, entering her house through the garage after making sure the door had lowered. Making up her mind to visit the neighboring house in the morning, she dropped her purse on the kitchen counter and removed her coat. As she did so, the odd scent assailed her nostrils, and her anger returned to mingle with grief. Grabbing a wire coat hanger from the small closet near the front door, she took the offending garment into the garage. She'd hang it there for the night She didn't want it in the house.

Maybe whatever that smell is will repel any spiders that might be hiding out here, she thought, looking for a bright side to the past hour as she fought off sadness.

Returning to the kitchen, she wondered briefly if she should phone Nadine, since they had just been talking about Hazel, but the news was too raw and Beryl's own questions as yet unanswered. She made herself a cup of tea, sat at the low counter which separated kitchen and living areas, and wondered what could have happened to her neighbor. She seemed healthy enough last month. Although Beryl knew George and Hazel Bennet had been very close and dependent on each other, she found it hard to believe that Hazel could have been so grief stricken over the loss of her spouse that she'd faded away in a month's time.

Beryl thought back to when her own Michael had been killed. The accident happened nearly 50 years ago. She had loved him unreservedly, but had she been so despondent that she'd nearly died? She couldn't remember.

Chapter 3

Beryl slept poorly that night. Floating in a half-sleep, she dreamed of Michael standing together with Hazel and George Bennet. Of course, Michael was long dead by the time Beryl had met the Bennets, but that wasn't the only strange thing about her dream. Beryl was with them on a battered wooden dock as the others were about to step into a leaky rowboat, but she was a little distance away, as if watching but still part of the action. She tried to speak, warn them that the boat would sink, but her throat constricted. She could emit nothing but a faint squeak. She wanted to run along the pier and warn them about the unsafe vessel, but her feet and legs wouldn't move fast enough. She felt as if she were wearing 50-pound shoes. She struggled to move forward, trying to reach them, and woke with a start when she sat bolt upright in bed.

Several seconds passed before the fog cleared from her mind and she was able to recognize her surroundings. She was cold and clammy, and her heart beat rapidly. Dropping back onto the soft down pillow and pulling the puffy green comforter up to her chin, she stared at the ceiling until her heartrate calmed.

Although it was only 4:48 by her bedside clock,

she knew sleep wouldn't return. Rolling out of bed and wedging her feet into blue furry slippers, she pulled on a thick terrycloth robe. She'd bought the wrap at a hotel during a business trip. The rare opportunity to travel and fill in for her boss had been both successful and fun. The robe was a memento. That had been years ago, but she clung to the memory as she shuffled into the kitchen to start the coffee. She didn't want to think about the nightmare.

While she waited for the machine to brew, she perched on the cushioned chair at the kitchen counter. Despite her efforts to banish the recent dream from her mind, her thoughts gradually strayed back to her earlier years with Michael. She had grown old, but the man in her dream was still the 35-year-old, vital guy she'd married. Forty-six years later, the dull ache still returned when she thought of him and what might have been, if not for the boating accident.

Michael had been a cop. Ten years on the force with a recent promotion to the detective division. The irony was he wasn't on the job when he was killed. He was water skiing with two old high school buddies. They were in the boat. He was on the rope and crossing the wake when a drunk college kid, joy-riding with friends in his brand-new speedboat, came out of nowhere, going much too fast. Michael's buddies said he never knew what hit him. Beryl hoped it was true.

She'd been 32 and unemployed. Although she could have lived for a year or two on Michael's life insurance, she needed the distraction of a job. With a high school education and a solid work ethic, she gained an entry-level position as dispatcher for a trucking company. Crossfern Shipping was a start-up with three panel trucks and a flatbed, running local routes.

Beryl grew with the company, ending a 40-year career as vice president and special assistant to the owner. He'd appreciated her hard work and devotion, rewarding her handsomely. During those years, she'd dated, received several marriage proposals and had even tried living with one of her lovers for a few years, but no man ever convinced her to remarry. She'd been retired now for six years and had no financial worries, but neither did she have expensive habits or hobbies. Her last male companion had died a year ago after suffering a stroke.

Beryl's reverie was interrupted by the coffee maker belching the last of the steaming water through the Colombian grounds. She pushed herself up from the chair to pour her first cup of the morning, and her thoughts turned to the previous evening. What in the world had happened to Hazel?

Beryl hadn't known her neighbors well. Didn't think anyone at Sunnydale did. The Bennets had bought the two-bedroom bungalow next door to Beryl after George retired nearly three years ago. During that time, Beryl and the Bennets had been friendly, waving and saying hello when they spotted each other, even chatting outdoors for a few minutes on extra-nice, sunny days; but Hazel and George appeared to be very private people and mostly kept to themselves. Whenever Beryl spotted the couple entering or leaving their home, they'd be holding hands or Hazel's arm would be tucked under

George's elbow. Those gestures always made Beryl smile.

She thought she might have gotten to know the Bennets better if they'd used their back patio, but for some reason, they didn't, not even to grill. Early in her acquaintance with her neighbors, she wondered if one or both might have allergies that prevented them from spending time outside.

Since Beryl's house was on the end of the row along the southern border of Sunnydale, the Bennets were her only neighbors on the row. The small yard of the cottage at right angles to hers, the first along the western side of the property, was hidden from her view by a blue spruce, sufficiently large to provide a screen and prevent patio-to-patio socializing. She enjoyed the peace and quiet of her tiny terrace that also afforded access to activities at the Big House, a short walk across the manicured lawn to the community's main courtyard, if she cared to join in.

Sitting at the low kitchen counter, looking across the living room and out the sliding glass doors, she was not studying the landscape now as the rising sun cast early morning shadows. She was looking inward, picturing Hazel as Beryl had seen her neighbor during George Bennet's funeral. Such a sad story, Beryl thought. They'd lost their only son less than a year before George's passing. Some families seemed to be jinxed.

Absently taking a sip from her mug, Beryl recoiled at the coldness of her coffee and stood to refresh her cup. As she padded across the kitchen, the door to the garage caught her attention and her mind flashed on the coat. She set her mug next to the machine and stepped into the garage. She'd hung the coat on the handle of a cupboard door. Its peculiar odor was faint, but still discernable.

She studied the black garment for a few minutes while her annoyance grew. The more she looked at it, the angrier she got as she realized whoever swapped this coat for hers had known exactly what they were doing. The shape of the collar was different. Her collar had been rounded, not pointed at the tips. She saw, too, not only was the collar dirty and frayed, but so were the cuffs. In the soft light of the theater and in the confusion of last night, she hadn't noticed some of the subtler imperfections. Irritation flushed her cheeks as she realized she'd been duped.

She reached into the coat's side pocket and pulled out the wad of paper before returning to the kitchen. With a fresh cup of coffee, she sat back down at the counter. Smoothing each slip, she lined them up before her and, donning her reading glasses, studied them with an eye for detail. A minute later, she reached for the cordless phone next to the wall and dialed Nadine's number.

"Did I wake you?" she said upon hearing a mumbled "Hello."

"What time is it?" Nadine didn't bother to reply to the obvious.

"Who cares?" Beryl said hastily, after glancing at the stove clock that displayed 5:38. "Wake up and get over here. I've something to show you." She hesitated a heartbeat before adding in a more solemn tone, "and some news to tell you."

"What?" Nadine sounded slightly more alert this

time and a little alarmed, maybe in reaction to Beryl's serious announcement.

"You asked about Hazel last night …" Beryl began hesitantly, unused to breaking sad news. Realizing there was no gentle way, she took a deep breath and blurted, "She passed away last night." When Nadine hadn't responded for several seconds, Beryl said, "You still there?"

"Yes," Nadine responded as if in a haze. Beryl could hear Nadine's intake of breath before her friend continued. "Was she that ill?"

Beryl described the scene that she'd encountered when she'd gotten home and ended by admitting, "That's all I know. Maybe Doe will come by later today and let me know what happened." Then, wishing to change the subject, Beryl said, "I've also been examining that coat I was given last night. You've got to see it."

"Why?" Nadine asked. "Did you find out to whom it belongs?"

Ignoring the precise grammar, Beryl said, "It's not mine."

"We already knew that," Nadine said, a touch of irritation creeping into her voice.

"No," Beryl said, "I mean it isn't even similar to mine. I was looking at it again and it's totally different." Thinking over what she'd just said, she tried again to explain. "That coat is a lot older than it looked last night in the dark." When Nadine didn't reply at once, Beryl threw out a temptation. "I'll make breakfast. How does a spinach-and-cheese omelet with crispy bacon sound?"

Nadine issued a short, cheery laugh. "You do

know the way to my heart, Beryl. Put the coffee on. I'll be over shortly."

"Shortly" turned out to be nearly an hour later, but Nadine looked freshly scrubbed and wide awake.

"Okay. What is it that couldn't wait?" she said, entering the living room from the patio. The walk across the lawn was shorter than going around by the road. When expecting company from the Big House, Beryl would unlock the sliding glass door.

Ushering Nadine into the garage, Beryl pointed out the flaws she'd discovered in the coat. "My theory is," she said, "whoever this coat belongs to took mine on purpose. Mine was brand new. Obviously, the thief wanted to trade up and I don't think she intends to return my coat. We're going to have to track her down."

With those words, Beryl led Nadine back into the kitchen, filled her cup with coffee and motioned her to sit at the counter. "Take a look at those receipts while I finish cooking. See what you make of them."

Minutes later, Beryl placed two breakfast plates on the counter after carefully pushing the papers out of the way, but keeping them separate and visible. "Do you see what's strange about them?" she asked after seating herself in the chair beside Nadine's.

"Why don't you tell me," Nadine said, as she picked up a slice of bacon.

"Well, look here," Beryl said, ignoring her own breakfast and placing the fast food receipt alongside the grocery list. "Here's a receipt for a Big Mac Meal and '1 M Coke'. That means medium-size soft drink and fries." She tapped the grocery list. "One percent milk, yogurt and tofu, along with assorted fresh fruit and vegetables." She fixed her eyes on Nadine. "Seem strange to you?"

Nadine slowly nodded. "Okay. Let me see if I understand. Last night, we decided that the person who printed the words on the library receipt was not the one who wrote the grocery list, so maybe there are two people living together. Now you've found evidence of two very different food tastes which further points to more than one person." She frowned at Beryl. "But what does it mean? Do you think there are two women and both of them wear this coat?" She shook her head in confusion. "Possible, but how does any of this help to track down whoever took your coat?"

Beryl stared back, narrowing her eyes. "*Stole* my coat," she corrected, then added, "That's what we're gonna find out."

Chapter 4

Nadine picked up the library receipt and scanned it. "You can cross Sunnydale residents off your list of suspects."

"I haven't thought about where that thief might live." Beryl said. "What makes you think it can't be here?"

"The Big House has its own library." With a flourish, Nadine laid the slip back on the counter and gave Beryl a conspiratorial smile. "Pretty good detective work for a beginner, hey?"

Beryl laughed. "Think you're clever, do you? Well, just because we have a library doesn't mean someone can't borrow from the public one, too."

"True," Nadine agreed, feeling somewhat deflated. "Speaking of books, though, I'm going to my first meeting of the readers club at the Big House this afternoon. Do you want to come along? We could ask the members if they use the local library. If they do, perhaps we'll stumble onto our mystery enthusiast."

"Nah," Beryl said, directing her gaze to the papers. "You go. I'm not much of a bookworm. Never had the time. Movies and plays are my game." She rearranged the scraps on the counter while Nadine dug into the omelet. A minute later, Beryl looked up from scrutinizing the papers. "While you're asking questions about libraries and books, see what the gossip is about Hazel, will you? I hope to talk to Doe today, but in case I don't, maybe you can get some news through the grapevine. We never had a memorial service for George here at the center, so now it looks like we'll need to plan a double service, and I'd like to speak to Doe about that, too."

"What will happen to the Bennets' bungalow?" Nadine asked.

Beryl shrugged. "Stan has a list of people interested in the community. I'm sure it won't stay empty long." She raised her eyebrows with sudden interest. "Wanna buy it?"

Nadine sputtered a laugh. "Oh, no. Another move doesn't sound very appealing. I'm only just beginning to feel settled in my condo. I like being close to the activities at the Big House. I'm getting to know people and have even been invited to join a bridge group."

Beryl made a face. "Not for me, thank you very much. I never had the patience for card playing."

Nadine snickered. "That's very clever."

"What is?" Beryl scowled.

"Patience," Nadine replied, unable to hide her delight in the pun, even if it had been unintentional. "It's what the British call solitaire." When Beryl stared back blankly, Nadine turned to look at the clock display on the stove. "Goodness," she said, rising from her chair. "Look at the time. I need to finish reading the book club selection for the discussion this afternoon." Pausing briefly, she said, "May I help with the dishes before I go?"

"I got 'em," Beryl said, standing as well and picking up both breakfast plates.

"If you're sure," Nadine gave her friend a few seconds to change her mind before adding, "Thanks for breakfast" as she headed for the living room and sliding glass doors beyond.

Walking across Beryl's patio, Nadine looked over at the neighboring house and thought of the poor woman, dying so suddenly. Even though she'd never met the Bennets, she remembered hearing about the husband passing shortly after she'd moved to Sunnydale, and the son's heart attack just months before that. Such a tragedy for the family. She wondered if there were relatives other than the daughter-in-law and granddaughter whom Beryl mentioned. *Step*-granddaughter, Nadine reminded herself with a half-smile.

Her thoughts segued to her own loss. Roger had been gone ten months and four days now. She missed him terribly. They'd met 56 years before as freshmen in college and married five weeks after graduation. Considering all their years together, she wondered how long it would take for her to get used to waking up alone or eating solitary meals. She still found herself waiting for him to come into the room so she could tell him about the funny thing that happened to her that day. She'd loved hearing him laugh. He'd had a deep voice for a small man, five foot eight in his stocking feet. Nearly perfect for her, being only a few inches over five feet tall.

"Hi, honey."

Nadine's reverie was interrupted by the greeting as she reached for the handle to open the glass door into the atrium at the rear of the Big House. *Henry*, she thought with a sinking feeling. For some reason, Henry Slater had taken a liking to her from the first day she'd moved into her condominium. He lived on the fourth floor and had made friends with her son when Ralph had been carrying boxes up in the elevator. He thought Henry was a great guy, but Nadine figured the man was just an old snoop, always showing up at her elbow, startling her. She'd begun to peek around corners before walking down a corridor or into a communal room and yet he still managed to creep up on her.

Twice in the past few weeks, she'd turned back toward her apartment with the excuse of forgetting something when the elevator doors opened onto his grinning face. Both times, he'd offered to hold the car for her, but she insisted he not bother and hold up other passengers. He was nice enough, she guessed, but she wasn't in the market for romance and didn't remember how to flirt, even if she'd a mind to do so. She knew several widows in the building would give their eye teeth for the attention he lavished on her. *Particularly Clara Fairchild*, Nadine thought, hiding her smile. She didn't need him to think she was glad to see him.

She wouldn't be able to avoid him this time. He was opening the door for her and holding up a penny. "For your thoughts," he said when she frowned, perplexed.

That's Henry for you, she groaned inwardly, feeling not a little peevish at the triteness of the joke, but she lifted the corners of her mouth and simply shook her head. "Not worth it, Henry. My mind's a blank this morning."

"I'm on my way to breakfast. Will you join me?"

"No, thank you. I ate with Beryl this morning. Now I've got some chores to do." She was not going to mention the reading club and chance his showing up.

She was spared further conversation when a shrill voice trilled out, "Hen-REE." They both turned to see Clara Fairchild hurrying toward them, followed closely by Greta Hensley and Francine Gleason. The three widows always made a big fuss over Henry, but Clara was particularly fond of the gentleman who, at 76, was closer in age to Nadine ... a fact the nonagenarian had no trouble disregarding.

"*We*'ll join you for breakfast, Henry dear," the flamboyant matron cooed, slipping her arm through his and pulling him along. This morning, her matching outfit was red and black. A lacy red camisole showed beneath a black, plunging V-neck sweater and hung snugly over the waist of a red-leather skirt that ended just above Clara's knees. Her red shoe-boots sported black two-inch heels and black laces. Even the hoops dangling from her ears were festooned with red and black beads.

"Good *morning*, Nadine," Clara trilled over her shoulder as she led the group toward the dining room. She was obviously pleased at having snatched Henry away from the latest object of his affection.

"Good morning, ladies," Nadine said quietly to their retreating backs, aware that none of the women waited for a returned greeting. She stifled a giggle at Henry's kidnapping and silently thanked her saviors as she headed in the opposite direction, toward the elevators.

In her apartment, she spent the next two hours reading the last chapters of *The Book Thief* in preparation for the Sunny Readers Book Club which would meet at one o'clock. Closing the cover and noticing there was still time before the dining room opened for lunch, she decided to unpack another moving box. Ralph had placed the cartons along a bedroom wall, leaving the living room and kitchen area uncluttered and ready to receive Nadine's treasures. She'd taken her time setting up her home and was pleased to realize she had only a half dozen crates left to tackle.

One of the few remaining boxes contained Roger's camera equipment. His main hobby had been nature photography. He'd loved taking walks both in the city parks and on wilderness trails. Several years before his death, he'd swapped his old gear for a more modern digital camera with various wide and telephoto lenses and a carrying case that held a small camp stool and a tripod. Nadine had no idea what she would do with the stuff or why she hadn't given it to their son, but somehow, she couldn't bring herself to part with it. Not just yet. The sight of it brought back memories of Roger teaching her to use the new equipment. She'd enjoyed the lessons, but quickly realized she didn't have her husband's eye for composing pictures. She often returned to her handheld camera and left the more sophisticated technology to Roger. Perhaps she would take up the hobby again and hang onto those happy days. With a deep melancholy sigh for good times past, Nadine forced her mind back to the present.

Tearing apart the Velcro strips holding the canvas seat to the case, she sat beside the next box in line. Perched on Roger's little fold-up stool, she spent the next hour removing newspaper wrappings and setting the items on the carpet around her. In her usual manner, she then surveyed the pieces, taking time to decide whether to keep an item or return it to the carton for Ralph to haul away and save or dispose of as he saw fit.

Her apartment was small but so nicely laid-out, it felt larger than the 800 square feet she knew it to be. Entering from the corridor, to the right was a coat closet and on the left, folding louvered doors hid a stacked washer and dryer. Past the tiny foyer were the door to her bedroom and bath on the right and a large open kitchen on the left. A thigh-high counter, similar to the one in Beryl's house, served as Nadine's dining space and separated kitchen from a spacious living room that ended in a sliding glass door to the balcony. The outside space was large enough for two chairs, a table and a small grill. Although it was much smaller than the house she'd left, Nadine was quite pleased with her new surroundings.

Typically, she preferred to make a sandwich or heat a cup of soup in her kitchen for lunch, but today, at 11:30, Nadine closed the carton she'd been working on, stuffed newspaper into the two boxes she'd managed to empty, and headed downstairs. She was on a mission from Beryl to find out if the Big House residents knew of Hazel's death and, if so, what they were saying. By eating with the first wave of diners, she also hoped to avoid Henry who, she'd learned, worked out three days a week with a personal trainer. On those mornings, he didn't get to the dining room until nearly one o'clock. Nadine hadn't yet figured out his exact schedule, but hoped Friday was one as she stepped into the elevator.

In the dining room, she was in luck. Henry was nowhere to be seen, but Mabel Gladstone was sitting alone at a small table near broad windows overlooking the courtyard. She was reputed to be the biggest gossip at Sunnydale. Not only would she know about Hazel, if anyone did, but perhaps she would also know of someone in the complex who read mysteries. If Nadine could find one "suspense" buff to look at the library receipt found in Beryl's coat, that one reader might lead to others until, eventually, Nadine was certain she could find the library patron who had checked out the old novels. With a feeling of smug satisfaction at her newly-acquired sleuthing skills, she gave her lunch request to the white-coated attendant at the counter, then strolled toward the preferred tables along the outer wall, mostly occupied even at this hour.

When Nadine first moved to Sunnydale, she'd once made the supreme mistake of choosing the table toward which she was now headed. Not only did she pick the ideal table, she also happened to sit in the choice seat. That particular mealtime, Mabel had been delayed at a doctor's appointment, so had been late in arriving for supper. Nadine had barely begun to eat when she felt a presence over her right shoulder seconds before hearing the voice.

"You're sitting in my chair."

Nadine put her fork on the plate, dabbed at her mouth with a napkin and turned to face her accuser. Startled to find herself nearly eye-to-eye with the woman without having to raise her chin more than an inch or two, Nadine took a few seconds to respond. "I'm sorry, but I didn't realize seats were assigned," she said, feeling both annoyed and embarrassed.

"They aren't," Mabel had stated with no hint of apology, "but everybody knows I always sit here." She was squinting at Nadine and talking overly loud, which Nadine later learned was because the poor woman was both near-sighted and hard of hearing. Narrow through the shoulders and broad in the hips, Mabel stood resolutely, arms folded across her chest and mouth pursed in disapproval.

Nadine realized if she were to fit in and get along with her fellow "inmates," as she'd heard some jokingly refer to themselves, she would have to pick up her partially eaten dinner and move to another table.

"You don't have to leave," Mabel assured Nadine as the latter looked around to find a vacant spot. "I don't mind if you share the table with me. Just move over there." As she spoke, Mabel carefully slid Nadine's tea cup to the opposite side of the table. She then swapped Nadine's full water glass with an empty one. By the time Mabel was reaching for the utensils, Nadine quite got the hint and gathered up her own place setting. She backed up and carefully skirted the table while Mabel quietly and efficiently laid down her clean setup. All tables in the dining room were designed for four. Nadine chose to sit diagonally across from Mabel while she finished her meal in silence and Mabel occupied herself by gazing out the window at the residents who were enjoying cocktails before coming in to eat.

This day, the supreme gossip was already seated for lunch and lifted a hand as Nadine came close enough for the vision-impaired woman to recognize her.

"Hello," Mabel called out, as Nadine had hoped she would. "Will you join me?" As soon as Nadine took the chair opposite, Mabel said, "It seems ages since we've talked. Are you all settled in?" The woman practically gushed, Nadine thought with an inward smile, knowing she would be pumped for every bit of information Mabel could glean. After all, that's what Nadine intended to do to Mabel.

They chatted amiably for several minutes until a server brought their requested lunches. As soon as he was out of earshot, Mabel looked surreptitiously around the room, leaned over the table and said in a loud whisper, "I noticed you coming from Beryl Fishen's cottage this morning. Tell me now, is the rumor true? Did Hazel Bennet pass on last night?"

Nadine knew of no reason why she shouldn't impart what little she knew to Mabel which was pretty much that yes, Hazel had died the night before and no, she didn't know the cause. Nadine finished by asking a question of her own. "Whoever told you the rumor, did they mention a cause of death?"

Mabel shook her head. "No, but I can ask Henry when he comes in for lunch. He was a great friend of George's, you know." She took a bite of chicken salad and laid down her fork. Her eyes twinkled when she said, "You won't mind him joining us, will you?"

After the initial jolt of delight at learning a tidbit for Beryl, Nadine's heart sank at the thought of dining with the man, but she hoped her face didn't show her annoyance when she answered. "Of course not, although I'll probably have to leave early. I'm going to my first meeting of the book club and I wouldn't want to be late."

"Of course not," Mabel parroted Nadine. Leaning over the table and seeming to suppress her excitement, she again spoke in a loud whisper. "Has Beryl told you of his late-night visits?"

Nadine felt shock stiffen her spine. Remembering some of the conversations she'd had with Beryl when they'd joked about Henry's attempted conquests, she felt color suffuse her face. Why hadn't Beryl mentioned anything about his visiting her? Had she and Henry discussed and laughed at Nadine's comments? Certainly not. Nadine was quite sure Beryl wasn't that sort of friend.

Mabel's voice interrupted Nadine's apprehensions. "I've seen him, you know." Mabel smirked and gave a curt nod. "Not just once, either." She bobbled her head at Nadine as if to encourage questions or speculation … or perhaps Mabel was fishing and expected Nadine to confirm the old gossiper's theory.

Watching the woman's squinty eyes reminded Nadine of the reports that besides Mabel's hearing problem, the woman had bad eyesight. She usually wore her hearing aid, the better to overhear conversations, but she often refused to put on eyeglasses. With that thought, Nadine experienced a surprising sense of relief that Mabel might be wrong about Henry Slater visiting Beryl. Certainly, she and Beryl had become friends enough that Beryl would have mentioned something to Nadine. She wondered again if Beryl kept the relationship quiet because Nadine had scoffed at the unsubtle advances Henry had been paying to her? Once more, she felt her cheeks grow hot at the thought she might have offended Beryl with some inappropriate remarks.

"You know," Mabel's stage whisper interrupted Nadine's concern, "Clara's furious with you."

Nadine nearly choked on the sip of water she'd just taken. Once she caught her breath, she said without trying to hide the anger in her tone, "What makes you say that? I certainly have had no indication of ill will between us."

"Henry likes you," Mabel said with another firm nod of her head, as if the reason sufficed.

"I think you're mistaken about Clara," Nadine insisted and was about to protest her innocence in encouraging Henry when she was interrupted.

"Hush," Mabel hissed as her eyes flicked beyond Nadine's shoulder. "Here he comes. I'll tell you later."

"Ahhh, two of my favorite ladies," came a voice close behind Nadine. "Mind if I join you?" The man himself appeared in Nadine's view, bent to kiss Mabel's upturned cheek, then turned toward Nadine.

She stood abruptly, putting the chair between them. "Please. Take my seat. I've finished and have an errand to run." With that, she flicked a smile at two stunned faces and spun away.

Chapter 5

Nadine left the dining room earlier than she'd intended, so she had nearly 45 minutes to kill before her meeting. Wandering toward the elevators, she stopped at the bulletin board where daily activities, programs and special events were posted. A large notice was tacked to the center declaring SAFETY PRESENTATION TODAY AT 2:30. Reading the smaller print, she saw that members of the local police and fire departments would be speaking to the residents and had a special announcement to make. All residents were urged to attend this important meeting.

With time on her hands, she returned to her apartment to phone Beryl. One thing the two women agreed on wholeheartedly was "no cell phone." Beryl said she'd spent enough years tied to a pager or BlackBerry during her business career that she wouldn't have another device going off in her purse, now that she was retired.

Nadine saw no reason to carry a phone. A few years before his death, Roger had purchased a mobile for no other purpose than phoning Nadine or their son Ralph whenever the fancy struck him. Having to drop whatever she was doing to answer Roger's calls from the golf course or from his car when he was stuck in traffic began to grate on Nadine's nerves.

One day, Roger unintentionally left his phone on the kitchen counter before settling down to watch a football game. Nadine was just lifting their dinner casserole out of the oven when both kitchen phone and cell began to ring. The cacophony startled her into dropping the hot dish. Ignoring the chicken and rice splashed across the floor, she picked up the cell and dropped it into the sink of tepid, dirty dish water before lifting the wall phone receiver and slamming it back in its cradle. She then raced to the bedroom where she slammed the door so hard, the house shook. No word was spoken, but when she finally emerged, the kitchen floor was spotless and there were no dirty or broken dishes in sight. That evening, Roger took her to dinner at one of the finer restaurants in town and never purchased another cell phone.

"If you want a callback, leave a message," commanded Beryl's voice when the recording cut in on the fourth ring. Nadine shook her head, amused. The first time she'd heard the message, she'd asked Beryl about its abruptness to which Beryl had replied, "Don't see the point in saying 'I' or 'we' are sorry to miss your call. One gives away the fact I live alone and the other is a lie. It seems silly to repeat my phone number. Whoever is calling has just dialed it. It's also totally unnecessary to say their call is important or that I'll call back as soon possible because chances are good that it isn't and I won't. All that's left is to tell 'em to leave a message."

Typical of no-nonsense Beryl, Nadine thought, grinning to herself, and left word about the safety meeting that afternoon. She decided to save Mabel's gossip for when she saw Beryl, either before or after the presentation by the police and firefighters.

With time to spare, Nadine went to the bedroom. She intended to unpack another carton, but Roger's camera equipment caught her eye. Dragging the case onto the bed, she removed the body and picked out one of the lenses. She spent the next half hour recalling her husband's instructions as she poured over the equipment.

With sudden awareness of the passing time, she swiveled her head to see she had only about five minutes to get to her readers discussion group. Leaving everything on the bed, she took the stairs one floor down instead of waiting for an elevator. Anxious not to be late to the book club, she was surprised to be first to arrive in the small community room. She had just settled into a comfortable stuffed chair when a woman ambled into the room. Moving slowly and stiffly with the aid of a walker, she silently nodded at Nadine before maneuvering around to sit on the straight-backed, cushioned chair next to Nadine's.

"Imogene Parsons," she said, finally turning to speak to Nadine. "I don't think we've met. I'm in two-oh-two."

So far, Nadine had not had occasion to visit the assisted-living or hospice sections of the Big House, but she knew residents requiring special assistance had rooms on the second floor of the building's wings where they were readily accessible to the nursing staff, therapists and caregivers as well as administrators who had offices on the same level.

Before she could do more than introduce herself to Imogene, a commotion outside the room heralded the arrival of Clara Fairchild, Greta Hensley and Francine Gleason. More than once, Nadine had heard Greta and Francine referred to as Clara's "ladies in waiting."

Clara certainly was flamboyant, Nadine thought as the petite woman in red and black breezed to an overstuffed chair and, with an expansive gesture, pulled a novel from an oversized purse. Dropping the volume onto the side table at her elbow, she removed a spiral notebook from the bag. As she stuffed her arm back into the colorful tapestry carryall, she looked up at the two women opposite her as Greta and Francine each took a straight-backed chair to Clara's right and left.

"I see a new face today," Clara said, beaming across a low, wide table at Nadine before nodding a greeting in Imogene's direction. "Welcome to Sunny Readers, Nadine. As the most senior member of this group, I lead the discussions." Her tone was enthusiastic and musical as she continued without waiting for comments or questions. "Shall we get started, ladies?"

Nadine made mental note of the others in the room and wondered if the "group" consisted only of these four women. If so, she wasn't pleased with the lack of interest and decided to find out if the rest of the community simply wasn't interested in reading. Being an avid consumer and a lover of many genres, both fiction and nonfiction, she hoped she hadn't moved into a situation where there were only these few residents with whom she could discuss books and authors.

Apparently finding what she'd been fumbling for, Clara pulled a pen from her satchel before she dropped the tote beside her chair. She then squeezed her facial features into a look Nadine took to resemble sadness or regret as Clara placed the notebook on her lap and folded her hands on the top. "First, we'll take a moment of silent prayer for our member Hazel Bennet who is no longer with us in this world." She bowed her head and her minions followed suit.

Nadine wondered who had spread the news to the rest of the building's residents, but kept still as she lowered her gaze and thought of a woman she'd never met.

"Hazel Bennet wasn't just a member. She founded this book club." The hoarse statement came from Nadine's neighbor as soon as a rustle from Clara's direction brought all heads up. Ignoring the cold stare from the apparent leader of the group, Imogene continued explaining to Nadine. "She was a good chair, too. Stayed open-minded about every reader's preferences." Leaning closer toward Nadine, Imogene confided, "She enjoyed a good mystery."

As Clara glared at Imogene, Nadine thought she saw a flicker of annoyance flash in the pale blue eyes. The glimmer disappeared before Nadine could be certain, but she tucked the news to the back of her mind and determined to speak further to Imogene. She might be just the person to lead Nadine and Beryl to their as-yet unidentified library patron.

In a sweet southern-belle manner, Clara broke into Nadine's wanderings. "Hazel Bennet passed quietly in the night. For that, we are grateful, but her blessed release means, of course, that she will no longer be with us. In my experience, times like this provide a wonderful opportunity to move forward and change our focus." She paused briefly before speaking directly to Nadine. "She was a librarian before moving to Sunnydale, you know, and wished to encourage better reading habits amongst our residents."

"She was open-minded," muttered Imogene.

Switching her gaze to the woman, Clara's voice held a firm edge, as if to ward off any objection. "Yes, she was, but it is my intention, to upgrade the tastes of our group." At this point, Clara seemed to realize the paucity of attendees at the day's meeting. "Some readers seem to have lost interest since Hazel fell ill and hasn't been able to join us. I had intended to assume her role only temporarily, but now that we know she won't be back, well ..." Clara didn't finish the thought that she would be directing the club from now on. When no one spoke, she added with a tone of finality, "We shall all miss her." The sentiment sounded almost like an afterthought.

Nadine wondered if what Clara said was true about Hazel's "quiet passing" and how did she know? The woman's next words interrupted Nadine's thoughts before she could speculate further.

"Our selection for this meeting is *The Book Thief*," Clara said, opening her notebook. "This novel by Markus Zusak is about a young girl in World War Two." With that introduction, she proceeded to summarize the story as if nobody else in the room had read the book.

Within minutes, Nadine understood that the gathering was not the sort of book club she'd been used to before moving to Sunnydale, but more of a stage with Clara the main, if not the only, player. As the nonagenarian droned on, Nadine found herself being lulled into a stupor. To keep from dozing off, she opened her own small pad and began to write. Clara's raised eyebrows and nod signified her mistaken belief that her words were being saved for posterity when, actually, Nadine was jotting down the titles and authors of a different set of books.

Murder Most Foul by Agatha Christie had been the first thought that prompted Nadine to begin her list. While the books on the library receipt in Beryl's swapped coat were still fresh in Nadine's mind from the morning's breakfast visit, she decided to capture them. *Scales of Justice* was another she remembered, scribbling down the title with its author Ngaio Marsh. She glanced up briefly, knitting her brows as she searched her memory. She nearly laughed aloud at the pleased expression on Clara's face as the woman obviously thought her last words had been particularly poignant to catch a member's rapt attention.

Lowering her head over the paper, Nadine scrawled rapidly *Strong Poison* by Dorothy L. Sayers. Mentally running through the four queens of crime, she came up with the last author, Margery Allingham, but it took nearly fifteen more minutes before she remembered the title, *The Crime at Black Dudley*. That was the toughest one to remember because Nadine had no memory of having read anything by Allingham. She'd have to remedy that on her next visit to the library, she thought. Satisfied with her list, she raised her head to realize everyone in the group was looking at her.

"Would you like me to repeat the question," Clara asked in what Nadine considered an unnecessarily condescending tone.

"If you wouldn't mind." Nadine felt her cheeks redden. The others might think she was embarrassed, but she was angry. *The nerve of that woman. I'm neither a child nor a pupil of hers*, Nadine seethed inwardly.

"I asked if you think there was any irony in Liesel stealing books?"

Before Nadine could answer, Gretchen spoke up. "I think it was ironic that she seemed more hungry for books than for food."

Hungrier, not 'more hungry' Nadine thought. She was tempted to correct Gretchen, but replied instead, "In my opinion, she wanted to keep people alive by hiding their works and their words. Hitler was killing people, attempting to destroy them body and soul by also burning the books, but Liescl was saving them. I think, by stealing the books, she was defying Death."

The room fell silent on Nadine's last words. It was as if her idea either confused the other women or stunned them into silence, but Nadine had said all she was going to. She wished the meeting would end. Then, as if reading Nadine's mind, Clara made a show of looking at the black watchband on her wrist. "Our time is nearly up, girls. In keeping with our new focus, I'm declaring the rest of the year's selections obsolete, so we need to select a title or topic for next week's meeting."

Nadine purposely kept from looking down at the list she'd made. "Perhaps instead of a particular novel, we could talk about the four queens of crime and their impact on the mystery genre."

Clara's broad smile didn't reach her eyes when she spoke. "As part of our new focus, we are dropping mysteries, thrillers and suspense from our repertoire. Hazel was such a devotee, most of us in this room feel 'enough is enough.' We're concentrating on other genres now, Nadine," Clara replied with obviously false regret. She looked to her left and right as Greta and Francine murmured agreement. Turning her attention back to Nadine, Clara continued, "I believe *The Book Thief* was enough of a mystery to satisfy that category for months to come. Does anyone disagree?" She waited almost two heartbeats before concluding. "Okay, then. Moving along, I suggest we read something by William Faulkner. How about *As I Lay Dying*. It takes place in the South, you know. I think it's amazing that he wrote it straight out and never changed a word of his first draft." She looked right to left, smiling at her ladies-in-waiting, who murmured their approval with nods and quiet hand-clapping.

Nadine was seething, but hoped her feelings didn't show beyond the slight warmth at the back of her neck and in her cheeks. Was this woman that ignorant? Not only was *The Book Thief* a teen novel, it was historical fiction. And as for Faulkner's work, as a student of English literature as well as a high school teacher, she'd had to read and teach stream-of-consciousness type of writing, but it wasn't her favorite style for reading enjoyment. She would prefer more recent and relevant novels, but kept her opinion to herself. Clara was obviously in charge. The reason for the present group's size suddenly became clear to Nadine as she decided she'd not be attending future book club meetings.

When the other women stood and began to chatter before leaving the room, Nadine headed for the corridor. With only half an hour before the safety presentation, she decided to question Imogene about other mystery readers another time. Now, she wanted to stop by her apartment and try to reach Beryl again.

Nadine took the stairs instead of the elevator up one flight to her apartment and thought about the few details she had to report. Most significant, she thought was the fact that Hazel had not only been a member of the weekly book club and a mystery buff, but she had organized the readers, probably because she'd been a librarian at one time in her life. Nadine also understood that the borrowed books on the public library receipt would not have been Sunny Readers selections, at least not since Clara took over for Hazel.

The idea of a mystery turned Nadine's thoughts to secret trysts that segued into what she'd learned from Mabel at lunch. Were Henry and Beryl having a clandestine relationship?

In her apartment, she saw the blinking red light of her answering machine and pushed *Play* to retrieve the message. It was from Beryl. Disappointed at her friend's refusal to attend the safety meeting, Nadine redialed Beryl's number and was relieved when she picked up. No amount of persuasion could change Beryl's mind, however, and the conversation ended with Nadine agreeing to visit Beryl after the afternoon's special event.

With a little more time to spare, Nadine wanted to satisfy her curiosity before heading to the main conference room. In her bedroom, she put most of the gear back into Roger's case, but held back the three items she meant to use. She then attached the telephoto lens to the camera body and mounted the body to the tripod before stepping onto her small balcony. She set the tripod next to the railing and focused on Beryl's back patio. Panning slowly to her left, she sighted along the Bennets' cottage and continued to the next bungalow, at which point, her view was cut off by her balcony wall. She lowered the camera and considered for a moment. *Was Mabel correct that it was Henry she saw crossing the lawn late at night? If so, had he been going to visit Beryl and why hadn't she mentioned anything to me? If not to Beryl's, would he have gone to Hazel's at that hour?* Another thought suddenly struck Nadine. *Was Doe his target?*

Chapter 6

Alone with her thoughts after Nadine left that Friday morning, Beryl spent some time cleaning house while obsessing about the coat someone had swapped for hers. Was the person really so hard up that she had to shop at the cloakroom of the local theater? Or was the woman simply a thief for the pleasure of the taking.

Nothing "simple" about a person who intentionally grabs something that doesn't belong to her, Beryl thought, pummeling the pillows before yanking the quilt over them. She couldn't abide thieves, ever since burglars had broken into their home when she and Michael were on one of the two vacations they'd ever had during their all-too-short time together. The police had never apprehended the burglars who'd stolen, among other things, her mother's wedding ring and the pearl necklace she'd inherited from her paternal grandmother. Irreplaceable because of the sentiment attached to the jewelry, never mind that she and Michael were dirt poor and struggling to make ends meet.

As Beryl pondered over the coat's evidence which, admittedly, was scant; she thought about what Michael might have done and, with a feeling of superior satisfaction, powered up her computer printer that also served as a copier and fax machine. Carefully smoothing the papers out on the glass surface, she made copies of every scrap she'd found in the pocket. She figured the red-and-gold-foil candy wrappers would hardly lead to catching a thief … but one never knew.

Shortly after nine o'clock, she donned an old sweater jacket she kept for tending her patio flower pots, picked up the check-out receipt and headed to the local library. There, because she'd never heard of two of the authors, she looked up the book titles to verify what she'd suspected. They were, in fact, all mysteries. She might as well have saved herself the trouble she thought a half hour later, having had no luck in persuading the library personnel to provide the name of the patron who had been delinquent in returning four books. From the volunteer at the checkout desk, she had been passed to an employee who had, in turn, handed Beryl off to the branch director. All said the same thing … they were tasked with protecting the privacy of the individual.

"Tasked," for heaven sake, Beryl thought as she left the building feeling utterly defeated. *Now what?* Sitting in her car, wondering what her next step should be, she brightened. A visit to the Yancys was long overdue. She started the engine and headed for Georgetown, nestled in the Front Range of the Rocky Mountains. Forty-five minutes later, she pulled up alongside the white picket fence that surrounded Butch and Cicely Yancy's small, two-story house on a side road in the historic mining town.

The couple had moved to the quaint community 15 years ago when Butch retired from what he described as "a too-long career" in police homicide. Too knowledgeable and experienced to lose, he was still in demand as a consultant and constantly in touch with his old department. Most important to Beryl, Butch had been Michael's partner for the last seven years of the young detective's life. The Fishens and the Yancys had formed a lasting friendship during that time, a bond that had helped Beryl through the painful first years of widowhood and which, over the ensuing years, had solidified into a feeling of family.

Butch answered the door to her knock. A tall, powerfully built man, he pulled her into one of his wonderful bear hugs that always made her feel small … not easy to do considering Beryl's height and girth. Cicely wasn't home, he explained, leading Beryl into the kitchen. His wife had gone to Thornton to help with a colicky great-grandbaby. He motioned Beryl to a chair at the kitchen table where, for the next half hour, they sipped coffee and caught up on family news.

Getting up to refresh their mugs, Butch finally asked, "Okay, Missy, what brings you to our door this morning? I can tell when you've got something on your mind." His smile diluted the implied scolding that she'd been too long absent from their hearth.

Beryl grinned back. "You know me too well, Butch." Handing him a copy of the library receipt she'd made, she explained about the coat swap and about wanting to find the woman who was brash enough to do such a thing. "Do you think you could find out who belongs to the number on that slip?"

"You'd love to show up on her doorstep and confront the bandit, wouldn't you?" Butch said, giving her one of his low, rumbling laughs.

"You bet I would," Beryl said, enjoying the thought and Butch's obvious pleasure in her plan for justice.

"Not sure I can do that," he said, frowning at the paper in his hand. He turned it over and studied the back. "Anything significant here?" He held up the handwritten side toward Beryl.

She shrugged. "My guess is they have something to do with the mystery plots of the overdue books." She looked at him with amusement. "I'll be sure to ask her when we meet." As if only just realizing what he'd said earlier, she scowled. "What do you mean you're 'not sure' you can get her name?"

"Just what I said. It's illegal. I'm not sure recovering a stolen coat justifies someone compromising their job or my conscience." Butch glanced away, obviously unhappy at disappointing her. When Beryl remained silent, he finally conceded. "Let me think about it."

Leaving Butch a short time later, Beryl decided to take a detour to the grocery store, so it was after 12:30 by the time she returned home to find a note taped to her front door. *Off to Grand Junction. Can't find Smudge. Will you keep a lookout for him? Back next week. Doe.*

Pulling the note off the door, Beryl went inside and dropped it on the kitchen counter next to the papers from the coat before hanging her jacket in the closet. She then put away the groceries and set a kettle on the stove to boil water while she made a sandwich for lunch. As she worked, she thought about Hazel's black cat.

Smudge was an inside cat that Beryl had checked on about every other month when the Bennets would drive to Grand Junction to visit their son for a long weekend. Hazel didn't like leaving the cat, but if they wanted to see Steven, George and Hazel had to make the four- to five-hour drive to the Western Slope. To make the trip worthwhile, they generally stayed two nights. Only rarely did their son and his family make the trip to Arvada. After Steven's death and George's failing health, the Bennets no longer made the long drive, but surprisingly, Doe began to visit them once or twice a month. Often and even more surprising, Hazel had admitted to Beryl, Kelsey accompanied her mother.

Now, perusing the note again, Beryl was certain Smudge was hiding, but wondered why. Remembering one of the lengthier conversations she'd had with Hazel, Beryl mentally reviewed what her neighbor had said about Steven's wife. A registered nurse, Doe Martine had been one of Steven's attending nurses after his first heart attack. When he'd been released from the hospital, Doe quit her job and went to work as Steven's private nurse. The next thing Hazel and George knew, Doe had married their wealthy, widowed son. She was 15 years his junior, a divorcee with a 16-year-old daughter. They'd been married about three years or so when Steven suffered his second and fatal heart attack. That had been eight months ago.

Beryl had seen Steven Bennet and his family only to wave "hello" when they'd visited the older

Bennets, twice during summer months and again last Christmas. The family never seemed to stay longer than overnight before returning to their home on the western border of the state. Beryl wondered if the shortness of their stay had been Steven's choice or Doe's. Considering the frequency of Doe's visits to Arvada after Steven's death, the Bennets must have realized the reluctance to visit had been their son's. Beryl wondered how that made Hazel and George feel.

It was at George Bennet's funeral that Beryl had her longest conversation with the daughter-in-law and that had been hardly more than a brief greeting. Doe had attended with Kelsey who, by the time Beryl approached to offer her condolences, was heading for the parking lot. Beryl caught only a glimpse of the tall, sturdy blonde as she turned to wave quickly before lowering herself into a cab. Unapologetically, Doe explained that her daughter had to catch a plane. The aspiring actress was flying to Sacramento to audition for an acting opportunity.

"In my day, I was fairly sought-after for productions in Grand Junction and Aspen. Only amateur stuff, you know," Doe revealed, dropping her eyes modestly as she adjusted the lace collar of her beige blouse. "And now Kelsey's following in my footsteps. When she was picked to star in her *second* high school play, she caught the bug." Doe went on with obvious maternal pride, "Because of the caliber of the California cast, my daughter says this is her big break. If she gets the part … and she's certain she will … she thinks the troupe will be in New York City by Christmas."

At Doe's elbow, Hazel had shaken her head imperceptibly at Beryl, indicating doubt at this last pronouncement. Whether the subtle signal meant that Kelsey wouldn't get the part or that the play wouldn't end up off-Broadway, Beryl hadn't been sure.

"She'll have to wait until all auditions are over, of course," Doe was explaining, "so she's flying back tomorrow to spend a little time with her grandmother before we drive home the next morning." At this, Doe had turned and put an arm around her mother-in-law's shoulder before leaning slightly toward Beryl. "After we're gone, I'm sure you'll watch over my dear Hazel and see that she's okay."

That was the last time Beryl saw or spoke to her neighbor before she'd learned of the severity of Hazel's illness. Apparently, her condition had worsened a day or two after the funeral. Of course, Beryl had seen Doe and Kelsey coming and going during the past weeks, but she'd assumed that they simply had changed their minds about leaving for Grand Junction and were helping Hazel through her grief.

When Beryl visited her neighbor's home earlier in the week, she'd learned that Doe had returned to the Western Slope only twice in the previous month to check on her own home and business affairs, leaving Kelsey to attend to her step-grandmother. Beryl wondered why Doe hadn't called on her, as Hazel's nearest neighbor, for assistance. She still couldn't imagine what had overcome Hazel to the point that she had been confined to a dark room. *Why hadn't Doe admitted Hazel to the skilled nursing facility at the Big House?* Beryl mused.

The whistle of the kettle replaced the question in her mind with more immediate concerns. Pouring boiling water over tea leaves, she then carried the pot and her lunch plate to the counter. Settling in her chair, she picked up the sandwich, took a bite and began to chew as she casually examined the note from Doe that she'd left on the countertop. Suddenly, she stopped eating and set down the sandwich before reaching for her glasses next to the phone. She slid them on and grabbed the grocery list, placing it side-by-side with the note that had been stuck to the front door. Bent over the two, she studied them closely before finally straightening up with deep frown on her brow. She would swear the handwriting was the same.

Chapter 7

Beryl glanced at the clock. "Horse pucky," she muttered in frustration as she realized Nadine would be tied up with Sunnydale's book club for at least the next hour. She had to talk to someone. Had to verify what she was seeing. Could it be that the coat belonged to Doe?

Hoping Nadine was at least hearing some useful gossip about Hazel's strange illness or cause of death from the Sunny Readers, Beryl again studied the two slips of paper before reaching for the phone. As she did, she saw the blinking message light and hastily pressed *Play*. Discouraged to learn that Nadine left nothing more than a summons to a safety meeting, Beryl deleted the message before returning Nadine's call, optimistic that she might have skipped the book club and would pick up.

"No such luck," she muttered when Nadine's recording came on. In a snit over not being able to discuss her discovery, Beryl snarled, "I don't need to listen to the police give you safety tips. I know plenty of cops and could probably give the presentation myself." She was about to hang up when she felt guilty about her abruptness, but softened her tone only slightly when she added, "Thanks for letting me know about it, though." She ended the call, but before returning the receiver to its cradle, she speed-dialed the Yancys' number.

Butch answered on the fourth ring and, obviously having seen on his phone display who was calling, skipped the preliminaries. "I'm still thinking about it. Don't rush me."

Ordinarily, she would have given him a hard time over his incorrect assumption as to the reason for her phoning, but she was too excited about her latest find to waste time teasing. "I have something I want you to look at. If what I suspect is true, you won't have to soil your conscience by hacking into a library database."

"I had no intention of hacking anything." Butch sounded irritated. "Honestly, Beryl, sometimes you …" He had no chance to finish before she cut him off.

"Are you coming into town today?"

"Hadn't planned to," he responded. "Why?"

"I need a handwriting expert."

"That wouldn't be me."

"But you know someone who is, I bet," she retorted.

She heard an impatient sigh before he spoke. "What now? Beryl, if this is another of your wild goose chases, I swear …" He fell silent, probably realizing the futility of what he was about to say.

"It's not a goose chase. Really, Butch, I'm on to something." With those words, she proceeded to tell him about the note from Doe. "I'm sure she wrote the grocery list. I'd just like someone else to verify it," Beryl finally finished. "I don't want to confront her until she gets back from Grand Junction and we're face-to-face. In the meantime, if I can prove that she wrote this grocery list, she won't be able to deny taking my coat." She added under her breath, "Gotcha."

"That the coat belongs to her seems to be a big assumption," Butch replied, "based on nothing more than comparing a scribbled note to a grocery list."

Beryl didn't speak for several seconds as her jaw tightened. Finally, she said through slightly clenched teeth, "Granted, it's an educated guess, but a darn good one. Who else would have Doe's grocery list in her pocket?"

"Okay, okay." When Beryl heard the chuckle in Butch's tone, she realized not only how silly her question sounded but also how adamant she'd become about retrieving a coat. Hearing another muffled snicker, she knew he was baiting her.

"Darn it," she sputtered. "I'm not that hard up that I can't afford a new coat, but I'll be hanged if I'm going to let a thief take anything from me again."

"I hear ya," Butch said, amusement still in his voice. "So, what if you confront her and she denies it's her coat? What do you do then?"

Beryl paused to consider his question. She didn't like liars any better than she liked thieves, mainly because she had no defense against either. Without proof, it was just her word against theirs. Finally, she answered him. "If I can verify that the handwriting on the note is the same as on the list, I'll have proof enough that Doe won't be able to lie her way out. I'll have caught her red-handed."

There was a short silence on the line before Butch finally said, "I might know someone. He's not an official expert, but graphology has always been something of a hobby. If he says you got a match, you can take it to the bank." As Butch continued speaking, Beryl relaxed and even managed a smile in knowing she could always depend on her old friend. "I might as well drive down into town. It'll give me a chance to go visit my great-grandbaby. Since I'm doing you such a big favor, you can meet me at the park-n-ride in Olde Town in an hour."

"Deal," she said, hurriedly ending the call before he changed his mind.

Having time to spare before their rendezvous, Beryl decided to make a copy of Doe's note. She turned on her printer and as the machine warmed up, she thought she'd also make a copy with the note and the grocery list on the same sheet, providing a clear side-by-side comparison, in addition to the copy she wanted to keep with the backups she'd made of all the papers from the coat pocket. Once she'd finished duplicating everything three times over, the remainder of the hour seemed to creep by. Increasingly restless, she left early and arrived ten minutes before the agreed-upon meeting time. Bless the man. Butch pulled in and parked next to her not more than three minutes later. After examining the side-by-side copy she handed him, he agreed the handwriting looked similar and reached into his truck's cab to grab a cell phone off the dash.

Eyeing her while holding the phone to his ear, Butch explained, "I wasn't gonna set things up until I'd seen for myself." She was about to defend her credibility when he dropped his head to listen. After a brief exchange, he slipped the phone into the breast pocket of his red-plaid flannel shirt and nodded. "He'll wait for me, if I hustle my large frame right over."

Laughing at what she suspected was a cleaner version of Butch's friend's actual words, Beryl thanked him with a hug. She extracted a promise that he would call as soon as he received the confirmation they were expecting, waved him off and returned to her car.

The phone was ringing when she walked into her kitchen from the garage. Glancing at the caller ID, she saw it was Nadine and noted the time was 2:09. "Thought you were going to the safety presentation," Beryl answered without preamble.

"I am, but I was hoping you'd change your mind and come with me. The notice says they'll be making an important announcement and want all residents to be there," Nadine insisted.

"I'm waiting for an important call," Beryl lied, not exactly certain when she would hear from Butch. "You don't need to go to a meeting on safety. They're all the same. Like I said before, I can tell you everything they're going to say. Could probably give the talk myself." Beryl tried to keep the impatience out of her voice. "I discovered something this morning that you should see. I want your opinion."

"What is it?" Nadine's curiosity was obviously piqued.

"Can't tell you. You have to see for yourself," Beryl wheedled.

"Sorry." Nadine could be stubborn, too. "I'm going to the safety presentation. I'll see you when it's over." With that, she ended the call.

Heaving a sigh of defeat, Beryl replaced the receiver and glanced down at Doe's note. This time, she was aware of the message's content and not just the handwriting. *Can't find Smudge.* With more than an hour to kill before Nadine would arrive and guessing Butch wouldn't be phoning for a while … or if he did, he could leave a message … Beryl decided to head next door to see if she could spot Hazel's black cat through the patio doors. If she were in luck, Doe wouldn't have closed the drapes.

Beryl piled the bits of paper together on the counter before crossing the living room toward her backyard, already mentally searching the Bennets' two-bedroom floorplan, trying to figure out where the cat might be hiding. She assumed Doe had left food and water for Smudge, so she wasn't too worried about him being shut up in the house for a couple of days, but she was curious and concerned that Doe hadn't seen the cat. As she approached the neighboring house, Beryl was startled to see a tall, muscular young man stepping through the glass doors onto the patio.

"Joey?" she called out.

"Hey, Beryl," he responded before turning back to slide the panel shut.

She frowned, watching him search through several keys on a large ring. "What are you doing here?"

Before answering, he glanced at his watch. "Came over to check on the place," he said, glancing over his shoulder to give her a brief smile before trying a key in the lock.

She frowned. Doe hadn't been gone but a few

hours. "How come?"

He shrugged. "Just doing what I've been told." The key obviously didn't fit the door, so he resumed fingering through others on the ring. "The boss said to come over and see that everything was okay."

Joey Marconi, a good-looking man in his middle twenties, had been hired as an exercise instructor at the Big House. The corporate director of Sunnydale also had Joey doing various odd jobs when he wasn't needed in the workout and weight rooms. The job was perfect for the young man who was training and studying to take the police entrance exam. After learning that Beryl had been married to a homicide detective and that she still had connections in law enforcement, he gave her both preferential and deferential treatment.

"Did you see Hazel's cat when you were inside?" Beryl asked, watching him try another key.

This time, it fit, but before he locked up, he turned to shake his head. "I just took a quick look around. Didn't see a cat, but I wasn't looking for one." He glanced again at his watch. "I need to get back to the Big House."

"Can I take a look?" Beryl ignored his impatience. "Doe Bennet left me a note. She hasn't seen Smudge and I'd feel better if I could make sure he's okay. Shouldn't take long. I know a couple of the places he likes to hide."

Joey lost his smile and shifted from one foot to the other. "I don't mean to be rude, Beryl, but I really am in a hurry. The safety meeting's starting and I don't want to miss it." He furrowed his dark eyebrows and leaned closer, studying her face. "Aren't you going?"

She shook her head. "I want to find Smudge. It shouldn't take but a minute."

"I really can't ..." he began, then stopped and glanced nervously over his shoulder before lowering his voice as if anyone in the Big House could hear. "How about if I don't lock up until after the meeting." Still watching her face, he pulled the key from the lock.

"I don't want to get you into any trouble," Beryl objected, unconvincingly.

His grin returned and he gave another shrug. "I can handle the boss. Won't be a problem. This way, you can take all the time you need."

Beryl returned the smile and patted his arm. "Thanks, Joey. You'd better run now, so you don't miss anything." He didn't appear to notice the humor in her tone as he spun on his heel and hurried across the lawn.

Chuckling to herself at Joey's seriousness, Beryl let herself into the Bennets' bungalow and carefully slid the door shut behind her before proceeding through the house. The air smelled stale. She suspected the windows hadn't been opened in quite some time and wondered if it had been Doe's decision, rather than Hazel's, to keep everything closed up. A shame, really, since the place was comfortable and beautifully decorated in brown and beige fabrics with burgundy accents. Too bad to keep the house so dark and gloomy.

With a sigh of resignation over the baffling actions of some people, Beryl went first to check the laundry room, knowing one of Smudge's favorite safe places was behind the stacked washer and dryer.

No cat, but Beryl stood for a minute to examine the shelving George had built in the space saved by stacking the machines instead of installing side-by-side models. She'd admired his idea when she'd been in the house previously and particularly liked the rectangular box-like base he'd designed to keep the laundry detergent off the floor in case of a water leak. Slightly more than a foot deep, about the size and height of a standard stair tread, the raised platform was also the perfect spot for Smudge's food and water bowls.

Beryl decided not to read too much into the fact that both bowls were full and appeared untouched, reminding herself Doe had driven away only a few hours ago. As Beryl left the room, she made a mental note to speak to Joey about building similar shelves in her own laundry room. With that thought tucked away, she went next to the master bedroom and with much grunting, got on her knees to look under the bed, another of Smudge's sanctuaries. When she found no cat, she used the bed to push herself up from the floor. She then wandered through the rest of the house, searching carefully behind furniture and opening every available interior door in case Doe had accidentally trapped the cat inside a cupboard or closet. While her main thought was finding Smudge, Beryl kept an eye out for a full-length, black coat with silver buttons.

Before leaving the house, Beryl returned to Hazel's bedroom, only calling this time instead of kneeling to look under the bed. Still no cat appeared, but a photo in a silver frame on the bedside table caught her eye. Based on their looks, Beryl guessed the professional portrait of George and Hazel had been taken within the last five years or so. An embossed date on the bottom edge of the frame read *September 30, 1960.*

Must be George and Hazel's wedding date, she surmised. As she studied the picture of the gray-haired couple, an idea formed in her head. Certain that Doe wouldn't care, Beryl decided to borrow the photo and have a copy made for the memorial wall in the Big House.

Taking the entire frame in order to protect the photograph, she made another circuit of the house, noticing for the first time that there were no other pictures. None of Steven and his family and no others of George and Hazel. *Strange*, she thought until it occurred to her that Hazel might have kept albums instead of displaying photos on the walls or tables. As Beryl backtracked through the rooms and out to the garage, she called to Smudge with no success. Finally giving up her quest, she went back through the living room and slipped out through the patio doors with an increasingly uneasy feeling.

Chapter 8

Nadine tapped her ring lightly on Beryl's glass door before sliding the panel aside and stepping into the cottage. She'd thought several times since Roger's death that she should probably take off her rings, but they seemed such a part of her after 56 years, her hand felt strange without them.

"Hello," she called out, just before she spotted Beryl waving her into the kitchen. Beryl's other hand held a phone to her ear. Nadine unzipped her windbreaker as she crossed the room, draped the garment over a chair and sank into the seat next to her friend at the low counter.

As soon as Beryl ended the call, Nadine was ready. She wanted to get her news in first. "You'll never guess who I ran into," she said, still feeling such a glow from her recent encounter that she ignored her own grammar rules.

"Probably not, so you'd better tell me," Beryl replied, returning the receiver to its charger.

"An old student of mine." Nadine stopped to correct herself. "I should say 'former' student because she's hardly into her thirties. A brilliant student. I always thought she'd go into medicine, but secretly hoped she'd teach." Nadine sighed as memories flooded back. "I imagined whatever career she chose would be a challenge, and I was right."

"One of the police officers at your safety meeting?" Beryl guessed, swiveling her seat to face her guest.

"Not exactly," Nadine responded with a feeling of pride. "She was at the meeting, even gave part of the presentation. She's a firefighter."

Beryl raised an eyebrow. "You don't say." Suddenly remembering the young woman who had broken away from the EMT group the night before, Beryl said, "Name of Jessica, by any chance?"

Nadine nodded and felt some of the wind leave her sails. "How'd you know?"

"Educated guess. I haven't seen many women in the local department." Beryl explained how she'd met the young woman and then felt guilty that she'd dampened her friend's excitement, so asked, "How was the safety presentation?"

"Oh, you know," Nadine waved a hand in dismissal, having lost her enthusiasm. "They told us about the latest scams against seniors and reminded us to be extra alert if someone asks too many personal questions or presents us with an incredible financial opportunity. You were correct. I've heard it before." She choked out a laugh, feeling some of her good humor return. "The main speaker even brought up the old saying, 'If it's too good to be true, it probably is.'" A little of Nadine's annoyance returned when she added, "Do you ever feel as if the older we get, the more we're treated like children?"

Obviously taking the question as rhetorical, Beryl asked instead, "What was the big announcement?" She was arranging and rearranging papers on the counter, impatient for Nadine to finish telling about her afternoon.

"Oh, yes," Nadine exclaimed, her excitement resurfacing. "I almost forgot. That was Jessica's topic. There's an arsonist in the area. Remember those three fires in the news these past couple of weeks? We talked about how close they were to Sunnydale, and you mentioned the coincidence that each house had been empty?" When Beryl merely nodded at the memory, Nadine went on, "Well, you were right. Each of the houses had a *For Sale* sign in the yard and each one had been vacated. Jessica said the fires were all started by the same person. The fire investigator apparently had identified an MO."

"And what is this arsonist's *modus operandi*?" Beryl interrupted, making certain Nadine knew what MO stood for.

Nadine shook her head. "She didn't say." She paused, frowned, and before asking, "Do you think it's one of those pieces of evidence they hold back? You know, so they can tell when they've caught the right person?"

Beryl snorted a laugh. "I keep telling you, Nadine, you watch too much television."

Nadine was beginning to realize that whenever Beryl avoided answering a question directly, it was because she didn't know the answer. Instead of voicing her suspicion, however, Nadine returned to the topic of the arsonist. "Jessica asked us to keep an eye out and report any strangers we see lurking around." Nadine had the distinct impression that Beryl hadn't even heard her last comment. Somewhat irritated, she decided to leave as soon as she found out what Beryl thought was so important. "What did you want to show me?" she asked abruptly.

As if she'd been waiting for the cue and, therefore, hadn't noticed her friend's pique, Beryl pushed two pieces of paper along the countertop in Nadine's direction. "Look at these and tell me what you see."

Nadine saw immediately that one was the grocery list she'd seen that morning. The other was a note signed by Doe Bennet. Nadine was about to shrug and slide them back when she looked closer. She studied them for several seconds before raising her eyes and her eyebrows at Beryl. "The handwriting looks the same. Did Doe write this grocery list?" Her eyes got wider. "Is she the one who took your coat?"

"That's what I think," Beryl said with a satisfying nod of agreement. "I gave a copy to Butch Yancy. That was him on the phone when you came in."

Nadine mentally heard fingernails screech down a chalkboard as she silently rephrased *That was* he *on the phone* …

Seemingly unaware of any grammatical gaffe, Beryl continued, "He called to confirm that his friend who studies graphology for a hobby is sure the same person wrote both the grocery list and the note."

Nadine examined the two bits of paper for another several seconds, then straightened and pushed the papers back to Beryl. "Okay, so Doe wrote these, which means the coat belongs to her, but why would she swap it? You've never given me the impression she was hard up." Before Beryl could reply, Nadine asked, "Where is that coat? Have you gone over it for labels? Anything that might have a name?"

"I hung the coat in the garage. Don't want it in the house. To answer your other question, yes, I've checked. There are no labels that say 'This coat belongs to Doe Bennet' or any other useful tags. Anyway, the coat's pretty old. It's probably been in at least one rummage sale, from the looks of it. I can't imagine Doe wearing something like that, but this note she left me matches up with the list found in the coat pocket. So what would you deduce from that?" She narrowed her eyes at Nadine. "Also, I don't think a person necessarily needs to be impoverished to steal, do you?" As she spoke, Beryl gathered up the rest of the paper scraps from the coat's pockets, patted them into a neat pile and placed Doe's note on top.

"Well," Nadine hesitated as she tried to solidify her reasoning. "I've only seen the woman from a distance and know only what you've told me about her, but you're correct … she doesn't seem the type to hang onto a coat that's so worn and shabby." Nadine squinted back at Beryl. "Besides, why would she be at the theater? Hazel must have been pretty bad off yesterday since she passed last night. If she was at death's door, I can't imagine Doe leaving her to attend a play."

After a moment's silence, Beryl's scowl disappeared. "Maybe my thief was Doe's daughter," she said, leaning toward Nadine with renewed excitement over the idea. "I'm sure she's in town." Beryl stopped, frowned, then corrected herself. "Or she was. Hazel's car isn't in the garage, so Kelsey must have been at the house today. I wonder why Doe didn't mention Kelsey in her note." Beryl stopped again and frowned as if puzzling out a thought. Nearly a minute went by before she spoke up. "As a struggling actress, Kelsey might buy her clothes at consignment stores. If she was in town, Kelsey could have gone to the theater last night. I wouldn't be surprised if she left the house to avoid having to help with a sick, elderly woman. If my impression is correct, as a struggling thespian, too poor to buy herself a new coat, she might just take a nicer looking one … or at least, not reject it if she was handed the wrong coat. That could explain Doe's list in the pocket."

Ignoring another impulse to correct Beryl's grammar, Nadine pressed her lips tightly together while she considered the possibility. Thinking back to the previous night's debacle, she said, "If she *were* at the theater last night, wouldn't you have noticed her?" She slightly emphasized the verb.

Seeming not to have noticed Nadine's subtle hint, Beryl shook her head. "Not necessarily. She might have arrived after the play started … or maybe she was backstage."

"How do you know she's in town? I thought you said she was off somewhere to audition for a part. Sacramento, was it? If she's staying next door, why haven't you seen her?"

Beryl chose to answer the first question. "Hazel's Ford isn't in the garage. That's why I think Kelsey's in town. She's the only one who uses that car … besides Hazel, of course." Beryl stopped talking and turned her face toward the living room, but Nadine could tell her friend wasn't looking at anything nearby.

"What are you thinking?" she asked, breaking the growing silence.

Beryl frowned. "If Kelsey was staying in Hazel's house, why would Doe leave me a message to watch out for Smudge? The Ford is missing, but I didn't see any evidence that someone was living there. No dirty dishes, no cosmetics in the bathroom … things like that."

"You've been in the house?" Nadine asked.

Beryl nodded and explained about searching for Smudge. "Don't tell anyone Joey let me in, okay?" she finished. "I don't want to get him into trouble with his boss."

Nadine gave her promise, then said, "Okay, assuming Kelsey returned from wherever she's been, how will you find out if she was at the theater last night?"

Beryl shrugged as if the answer was obvious. "I'm going to the theater tonight and talk to Tish Nanquette. If Kelsey is as ambitious as I think, she'll have introduced herself to the local theater manager and made herself known every time she was in the place. Makes sense to ask, anyway." As if her plan needed no further explanation, Beryl changed the subject. "What was your question?" she asked.

Disoriented by the non-sequitur, Nadine tried to reorient herself. "What question?"

"You said you had something to ask me, something personal," Beryl reminded her.

Nadine felt her cheeks grow hot as she hesitated over prying into her friend's love life. Beryl waited until eventually Nadine blurted, "Are you seeing Henry? Has he been visiting you at night?"

Beryl simply stared at her friend with widening eyes for several seconds before she burst into laughter. "You're kidding, right?" she finally sputtered.

Feeling somewhat foolish because of her friend's reaction, Nadine shook her head. "No, I'm not kidding. I had lunch with Mabel today and she said she saw Henry walking over here ... late at night ... more than once." With each added phrase, Nadine felt her cheeks grow hotter. Was she being as absurd as Beryl's amusement seemed to suggest?

"I think Mabel had better have her eyes checked," Beryl said, chuckling. "If Henry Slater ever found courage enough to come to my door in the middle of the night, I'd send him packing." She gave a snort of delight again. "I can't believe you think I'd have anything to do with that man." She fluttered her eyelashes at Nadine. "Besides, everyone knows he only has eyes for you."

"Really, Beryl," Nadine exclaimed, feeling her face glowing rosy, "we both know Henry's advances mean nothing."

"So why do you think I'd be interested in him," Beryl asked and snickered as Nadine squirmed.

"I'm sorry I listened to Mabel," Nadine blurted, wishing she'd never repeated the gossip. "I should have realized that Clara would have been right on his heels, chasing him across the lawn, if he was having a tryst with another woman."

At the image, both women fell into such a fit of laughter that tears ran down their cheeks. Finally, Nadine grabbed a nearby paper napkin to wipe her face and gasped, "Speaking of Clara, I think you'd like to hear about the Sunny Readers." She knew Beryl wasn't much interested in the book club, so figured she was being a good sport when she agreed.

"First," Beryl said, glancing over at the digital clock on the stove, "it's as near to five as makes no nevermind," using an expression Nadine hadn't heard since her grandmother had passed away. "I think we might need something a little stronger than tea before you fill me in."

While Beryl rose to open a bottle of wine and pull goblets from the cupboard, Nadine fished in her pocket for the small notebook she'd had at the afternoon meeting. Giving a sigh and speaking mostly to herself, she said, "Now that you probably know who has your coat, there seems to be no need to follow up on the library receipt."

Beryl returned to her seat at the low counter with a bottle of Merlot and two wine glasses. Either she hadn't heard or was ignoring the last comment as she poured and handed one of the glasses to Nadine. "Skoal." Lightly touching the rim of her goblet to Nadine's, she took a sip and settled herself in the high-backed chair. "Tell me what you got, anyway. I'm all ears."

Nadine raised her glass in silent salute and took a small sip herself before filling in Beryl on the club's proceedings, including the discovery that Hazel had been the group's founder. "Did you know she'd been a librarian?"

"Had no idea," Beryl admitted.

Nadine opened the notebook she'd placed on the counter, unmindful of Beryl's less-than-enthusiastic tone. She'd gotten wound up over her memories of the afternoon and talk of books. "Since I looked up the titles, I'd like to share with you what I found. I think the plots are interesting."

"Fine," Beryl said, taking a healthier gulp of the Merlot.

"I'll start with *Murder Most Foul* by Agatha Christie," Nadine began. "In this story, the protagonist Miss Marple is the sole dissenting juror in a murder trial of a man accused of killing an actress. The next one, *Scales of Justice* was written by Ngaio Marsh about the murder of a colonel, an avid fisherman, in charge of publishing a controversial memoir." Nadine looked up from her notes to explain, "Marsh was a theater director, you know."

"Really?" Beryl remarked as she sat straighter.

When reference to Marsh's other passion caught Beryl's attention, Nadine suspected her friend had been only half listening to the plot descriptions. She guessed the other half of Beryl's mind had probably been considering her visit to the local theater and the upcoming confrontation with Tish Nanquette.

Nadine nodded before resuming her recitation. "In *Strong Poison*, Dorothy L. Sayers' character Harriet Vane is accused of murder. The murderer gives arsenic to the victim after having built up an immunity by taking small doses over a long period. Finally, *The Crime at Black Dudley* by Margery Allingham is about a group of house guests held captive by a gang of crooks." Looking up as she closed the pad, Nadine asked, "How do you suppose the words written on the back of this receipt are connected to these stories?"

"Don't know," Beryl said, raising an eyebrow. "Guess we'll have to ask Kelsey when she returns my coat." As if wishing to drop the sore subject, she tipped her chin at Nadine's glass. "You've hardly touched your wine," she observed. "Would you like cheese and crackers to go with it?" She turned to look at the stove's digital clock that displayed 5:27. "Or maybe a quick supper? The performance doesn't start until seven tonight, so I thought I'd catch Tish Nanquette about six-thirty. Still plenty of time to whip up some supper first."

"Sorry, Beryl. Can't." Nadine stood, preparing to leave. "I'm having dinner with Jessica. I want to hear what she's been doing since her high school graduation and why she chose to become a firefighter. We have lots of catching up to do."

Beryl was disappointed, but rose cheerfully to accompany her guest to the back door. In the living room, Nadine gathered her coat from the wingback and was slipping it on when her attention was drawn to a picture frame on the table beside chair. "Nice looking couple," she said, leaning in to study the gray-haired man and woman. "I haven't noticed this before. Who are they?"

"I forgot," Beryl said. "You never met George and Hazel Bennet, did you?" She picked up the frame and handed it to Nadine.

"No. George died not long after I moved into my apartment. If they ever came up to the Big House before his passing, we were never introduced." Nadine held up the picture to catch light from the kitchen's overhead fluorescents. "They were a handsome pair. I'm certain I'd have remembered meeting them. And what a lovely frame," she said. Playing a finger across the inscription at the bottom edge, she smiled over at Beryl. "How long ago was this was taken? Looks like some sort of anniversary celebration," she observed, handing back the photo.

"According to the date, the picture might have been taken at their forty-fifth." Beryl's tone sounded slightly melancholy when she added, "Michael and I only made it to ten."

Chapter 9

After Nadine left for the Big House, Beryl phoned the local theater to see if the manager might be in her office.

"No," replied the young voice to Beryl's question. "Mrs. Nanquette doesn't come in until after the intermission. I'm her assistant. Can I help you?"

If Beryl's impression of Kelsey was correct, she doubted the aspiring young actress would introduce herself to anyone except the person in charge. "No, thanks," Beryl said before hanging up. She believed her best plan of attack would be not to leave a message, but to meet Tish Nanquette face-to-face. Beryl would go to the theater and speak to Mrs. Nanquette near the end of the night's performance.

That decided, Beryl found herself with time on her hands, but with little appetite for supper. She heated leftovers in the microwave and ate standing up with her back against the refrigerator door. Putting plate and fork into the dishwasher, she settled in the wingback recliner and turned on the television to watch PBS NewsHour. The combination of food and monotonous sounds from the TV lulled her to sleep.

She awoke nearly an hour later as a good-news story was airing about a cat who had been returned to her owner after being lost for two years. Listening to the broadcast, Beryl began to wonder about Smudge. *Where could he be hiding? I went through every conceivable room and closet in the house*, she thought and mentally reviewed her trip through Hazel's cottage. Could the black cat have kept avoiding her while she was roaming through the house?

She remembered the game she'd played with Smudge the last time the Bennets had asked her to check on him. She'd covered the head of a flashlight with a piece of cardboard so only a tiny ray of light came through. It was a cheap way to simulate a laser beam without having to buy the real thing. The cat had delighted in chasing the light around the floor and up along the back of the sofa.

Joey had probably locked up the house again, Beryl mused, but maybe if she could play a light through the glass patio door and run it along the living room floor, Smudge might come out of hiding for the delight of a chase.

With the plan formed in her mind, she switched off the television and headed for the garage. There, she hunted through the recycle bin and picked out a cereal box. Retrieving a flashlight and tools from the workbench, she cut a cardboard circle to fit the lens. Using a Phillips-head screwdriver, she made a small hole in the middle of the makeshift cover before securing the disc over the light with a strip of clear tape. Satisfied with the narrow beam that had attracted the cat previously, she headed out of the house and across her backyard to Hazel's patio.

When she reached her neighbor's sliding door, she turned on the flashlight, but much to her dismay, the light simply reflected back at her. "Horse pucky," she hissed softly. "Tinted glass." In frustration, she tugged on the handle and was startled when the panel slid silently along the track. "Joey didn't lock up," she murmured, startled by the carelessness of the usually conscientious young man. *Probably got busy and forgot*, she thought, remembering his excitement over the afternoon's safety meeting. *I bet he got too distracted being around cops to think about Hazel's place. My good fortune*, she congratulated herself as she widened the opening, slipped quietly into the living room and shut the door behind her. The house was dark, but enough ambient light allowed her to move about without having to turn on the flashlight.

She headed to the laundry room, the site of food and water for the feline. As soon as she entered the room, she felt something was wrong. Then she saw it. The trap door to the crawl space was exposed. Had it been like that when she'd searched the house earlier? She couldn't remember, but she did know that Hazel always kept a wastebasket over the space. She had explained to Beryl that she was afraid the plywood cover was unsafe and might cave in if she stepped on it.

The crawl space, Beryl thought suddenly, shivering at the image. She hated going into her own dark cellar. The shallow spaces were always so cold and dusty, but that's where the furnace was located. She'd had to change her own filter a few times when she hadn't been able to find a willing friend or available handyman to do the job. If Doe'd had cause to go into the basement, Smudge might have followed. If she hadn't known he was down there, she might have accidentally trapped him. Worse yet, maybe she'd locked him in on purpose and her note asking Beryl to keep an eye out for the cat was to obscure the evil deed. Beryl mentally shook the last thought out of her head, scolding herself for the unfounded accusation, even if it was only a fleeting idea.

Deciding she had no alternative but to check, Beryl reluctantly pulled back the hinged trap door until the top edge rested against the wall. She switched on the flashlight, peered down into the hole and took a deep breath before beginning her descent. The dime-size spot of light was enough for her to ease her way down the few rickety wooden steps to the grimy floor. Hesitating on the bottom tread, she softly called out to the kitty while trying to rid her mind of the story she'd heard of the man who'd discovered four dozen black snakes in his crawl space after realizing the ground beneath his feet was moving. Shuddering at the thought, she ran the light along the area in front of her. No snakes, but that didn't remove the chill from her spine.

She quietly called again to the cat. She knew she needn't shout. Cats have acute hearing. When no answering sound broke the silence, she left the last step and played the beam back and forth without seeing any movement. Once on the grubby cement floor, she had to bend slightly to avoid banging her head on the beams. Unable to stand upright, she shuffled slowly ahead, searching side to side with the light. If Smudge were nearby, certainly he'd come to her.

She had taken a half dozen steps toward the

middle of the cellar and was about to call out again when a creak overhead stopped her cold. Frozen in place, she listened. Hearing nothing more, she was about to move forward when she heard the creak again. Someone was in the house, walking overhead … not just walking, but creeping slowly across what Beryl estimated to be the living room. Had that person been in the house when Beryl entered? She thought of the unlocked patio door. Was it Joey? Was he upstairs checking on the house? *No*, she disregarded the notion as another floorboard gave a sigh of protest. He wouldn't be sneaking around. Would he? Should she call out? Maybe Doe had returned. *Certainly she wouldn't be tiptoeing about either.*

With her back beginning to cramp and no sign of the cat, Beryl turned around to head toward the stairs and the relative light of the trap door when a sudden thought struck her. What if whoever was up there noticed the trap door was open and decided to shut it?

The thought that she could be locked in drove all caution aside. She opened her mouth to shout and let the person overhead know she was down there when she felt something brush against her ankle. Her shout turned into a high-pitched shriek and she jerked upright. The move brought her head into sharp contact with a crossbeam. Pain shot through her skull as she pitched forward, dropping to her knees. When she threw out her arms to break the fall, the flashlight flew out of her hand.

In the fear and agony that gripped her, Beryl was only vaguely aware of rapidly retreating footsteps.

Whoever had been lurking was now running away, but Beryl's attention was focused on escaping from whatever had attacked her. She looked frantically around for the flashlight and nearly cried for joy when she spotted a narrow beam almost immediately. *Thank heavens it didn't break*, she thought, scuttling forward to grab the torch. As her fingers touched the cold metal, something furry rubbed against her shoulder. She recoiled with a sharp shout, raising her arm to lash out. It was then she heard a soft mewing. *Smudge*. The wave of relief sapped every bit of energy from her body and she sagged to the floor. Several minutes passed before she was able to regain strength enough to roll to a sitting position. Disregarding the dirt on her clothes, she reached out and gathered the cat into her arms, nuzzling his fur as he rubbed his head against her neck.

As the knowledge sunk in that Smudge was safe, awareness returned and Beryl considered her predicament. She had to get out of the crawl space, up into the light and fresh air. Confident the cat would follow her, she set him down, turned onto her hands and knees, and crawled toward the stairs. The sight of Smudge scampering up the narrow steps ahead of her made her laugh aloud. She wondered if she was having hysterics and sobered quickly.

In the relatively brighter light and warmth of the laundry room, Beryl had second thoughts about entering the living room. Most immediate, she had to get rid of the feeling that a creature was about to jump up out of the cellar and grab her. As quickly and quietly as possible, she lowered the trap door and, almost unconsciously, moved the nearby wastebasket over the lid. Having taken care of one problem, she turned her thoughts to the rooms beyond the door in front of her. Who was out there?

Her mind whirred. *Who had been creeping around the house? Are they still here? Waiting for her to show herself?* Her throat constricted again with nervous laughter as she imagined her adversary hunkered down behind a chair. Was that person listening as hard as Beryl herself to hear sounds of another's presence? She pinched the skin on her wrist until the impulse to snicker subsided. She couldn't give in to hysteria.

Soberly, she tried to think what direction the retreating steps had taken, but her mind was fuzzy and her head was throbbing. To make matters worse, Smudge was staring intently toward the darkened room beyond the laundry door. Making up her mind to act quickly, Beryl scooped up the cat and dashed into the living room. Seeing the open patio door, she hesitated for half a heartbeat. Hadn't she closed it when she'd come into the house? She was certain she had, but didn't wait to question her good fortune. She ran out into the night, not bothering to slide the panel shut behind her as she headed for home. Whoever left the door open could close it themselves.

Safely in her own house, Beryl released the struggling cat. Smudge calmed immediately and began to groom his coat, as if to remove the human fingerprints that marred his fur. Beryl sat in her favorite chair and watched him, allowing her heart rate to slow. Back in familiar and comfortable surroundings, her mind relaxed and turned to practical matters. Smudge would need food, water and a commode of some sort, but she wasn't about to return next door. She would not go back into that house. *Not at night and not alone*, she told herself. *Who had been in Hazel's house?* she wondered again as cold, phantom fingers crept down her spine. Mentally scolding herself to stop dwelling on what could have but didn't happen, she returned to making a mental list for her new houseguest.

Of one thing she was certain ... a litter box was one necessity that couldn't wait until morning. Exhausted from her recent scare and activity, nonetheless, she had to go out again. She looked down at herself, noting her soot-stained tunic. The knees of her navy blue slacks were smeared with dust and the right leg was torn at the seam. "Horse pucky," she swore before her eyes moved to the grooming cat. Nothing for it but to go. She'd have to change her clothes, but she'd forego the shower, at least until after Smudge had his kitty bathroom.

Once she changed into clean slacks and a pullover, she picked up her purse and, heading for the garage, called over her shoulder, "Don't answer the door or the phone, Smudge. I'll be right back." She chuckled to herself as she got into her car and started the engine. How easily she'd fallen into her old habits of talking to her pets. When she'd lost her last cat two years ago, Beryl decided she might not outlive another. Having Smudge in the house brought back the sense of peace and happiness she'd experienced with her animals.

Her intended quick trip to the local grocery store took Beryl nearly an hour as she hunted for litter supplies and then tried to figure out which of the myriad flavors of canned or dry food Smudge might prefer. Did he need treats, too? Should she get the toy mouse or the catnip ball? Once she'd filled her basket, she'd stood in line behind four other people at the only cashier's line.

Eventually, Beryl left the store with an overloaded grocery bag of food, toys and treats, along with a 10-pound sack of litter and a blue plastic cat box. As she started the engine and glanced at the dash, she noticed with some surprise that it was nearly nine o'clock. When she turned onto the narrow road leading to her bungalow, her headlights picked out a dark sedan parked on the weedy strip opposite the houses. The unclaimed and untended strip along the road was generally where utility vans, maintenance trucks and residents' guests parked.

At this hour, whoever owned the black Honda must be a visitor, Beryl guessed idly. She would have dismissed the vehicle's presence and thought no more about it, except she saw movement on the driver's side. Although the head rest might account for the human-head-like silhouette, Beryl was certain someone had just slithered down in the driver's seat. Why were they trying to hide? Why just sit there if they were here to visit someone? *Unless they're up to no good,* she thought.

Beryl slowed and turned to look into the car as she passed. Sure enough, someone was slouched against the door as if they'd fallen asleep. The visor of a ball cap hid the face. Beryl couldn't tell if the person was male or female. With a mental shrug, she drove by and pulled into her garage.

For the next half hour, she was preoccupied with setting up her home to accommodate the cat. As these chores wound down, her mind returned to the mysterious car down the road. Curious, she opened the front door to see if the vehicle was still there.

When she saw the car had not moved, Beryl decided to investigate. *Could this be the person who had been skulking around Hazel's living room earlier?* she wondered. Surprisingly, she felt no alarm at the idea of confronting the individual and realized it was because she wasn't trapped in a dank crawl space. She would be out in the open and felt no fear of politely questioning the presence of a stranger.

For the 12 years she had lived at Sunnydale, the neighborhood had always felt safe, so she had no thoughts about phoning the police. Instead, she donned her sweater jacket and only then realized her flashlight was lying on the dirt floor of the cellar next door. Maybe Joey would retrieve it for her, she thought as she stepped out of her front door. The fall night was lovely and clear. She pulled her sweater tight against the chill and, momentarily, gazed up at the star-filled sky before heading down the sidewalk.

As she drew opposite the automobile, Beryl saw the driver bent over the steering wheel. Asleep? She crossed the road and knocked on the passenger window, noticing only then that the occupant was a woman. Obviously realizing she'd been caught, she turned at the tapping to smile wanly at Beryl. Almost immediately, the passenger window quietly lowered to reveal a familiar face.

"Jessica?" Beryl said, surprised to find the young

firefighter parked on the street.

"Hello," the young woman responded, looking decidedly sheepish at having been caught out. "Beryl, isn't it?"

"Yes," she acknowledged. "I thought you were having dinner with Nadine tonight."

"That's right. You and Mrs. Rodd … uh, Nadine, are friends, aren't you? She speaks very highly of you." Beryl could see the woman relax slightly, but she still looked on her guard.

Beryl never knew what to say when someone complimented her, so her reaction was to change the subject. "How come you're sitting here?" Beryl asked.

"I thought, as long as I was in the area, I'd keep an eye on the Bennets' place for a while."

Almost with a feeling of relief, Beryl said, "Were you inside about an hour or so ago?"

Jessica frowned and shook her head. "I've no authority or permission to enter the premises. Why do you ask? Did you see someone go into the house?"

To protect Joey and the favor he'd done for her, not to mention her own culpability for trespassing, Beryl decided not to confess to being in the house herself. Instead, remembering what Nadine had told her about Jessica's presentation at the safety meeting, she raised her eyebrows. "Ahhh, the fires." More seriously, she asked, "Do you think the arsonist will come here?" Silently, Beryl tried to clear her conscience. If the arsonist had been the person in Hazel's house, she'd certainly scared him away when she'd screamed.

Jessica shrugged. "Don't know, but I thought I'd

keep an eye out, just in case. If my fire-loving friend keeps to a pattern, I'm thinking he will strike somewhere either tonight or tomorrow night."

"Who knows this place is empty?" Beryl had convinced herself by now that Hazel's bungalow was not a target, and her tone made the feeling evident.

The young firefighter hesitated as if considering before answering. "Everyone who was at the safety meeting at the Big House this afternoon because the question was raised. The residents were very concerned. That's one of the reasons I decided to sit here for a little while."

"Do you suspect one of the Sunnydale residents is your arsonist?"

Jessica responded too quickly to reassure Beryl. "Oh, no. I didn't mean to imply that. But people talk to friends and relatives. You know how fast word can spread."

"Yeah," Beryl agreed, "particularly when a tragedy's involved." At that moment, she was doubly glad she hadn't revealed her presence in Hazel's house that night.

During her conversation with Jessica, Beryl had been bending to look through the passenger window. Feeling a twinge in her back as well as in her conscience, she decided it was time to return home. Before straightening, she said, "You're probably wasting your time, but if you're going to be here for a while, want some coffee?"

"Thanks, but no," Jessica smiled. "I might stay a little longer, but you're probably right. Nothing's going to happen here tonight."

Chapter 10

Beryl sat back in her recliner and idly stroked Smudge. With all that had transpired that evening, she'd completely forgotten about going to the theater to speak with Tish Nanquette. When she finally did remember, she had no desire to leave the house again. The woman wasn't going anywhere, Beryl decided. She would question the manager another time.

Curled in her lap, the black cat was purring softly, and Beryl began to doze. She'd had a long day, busier than usual, but she'd been too keyed up to go to bed. As she sat fighting off sleep for the moment, she thought back over the day's events leading to the discovery of the person who'd stolen her coat. How bizarre that the thief probably lived next door. Was it only last night that she and Nadine had gone to the theater's Thursday opening performance? It seemed more like a week had passed instead of slightly more than 24 hours.

Beryl thought of the coat she'd had to wear home and wrinkled her nose in disgust. She wondered if the owner had ever had the garment cleaned, and then a new thought struck her. Maybe the criminal recently picked it up at a garage sale and brought it to the theater with the express intention of swapping it.

Now who's watching too much TV, she chided herself with a chuckle. Forcing unpleasant images from her mind, she returned to petting the snoozing cat in her lap.

Sliding her hand over Smudge's silky back, she thought of "Miss Kitty," the last pet she'd had. The 18-year-old, short-haired domestic had passed away in her sleep two years ago. She'd had such a sweet disposition. Delicate and pretty, too. White with black and gray patches on her sides and crowning her head. She also had the most beautiful green eyes Beryl had ever seen in a cat. Drowsily, she studied the black feline in her lap and a sudden feeling of emptiness tugged at her heart. She hadn't realized how much she missed her cat. At that moment, she made up her mind to adopt Smudge, firm in the belief that Doe wouldn't object. As Beryl warmed at the thought of his staying with her permanently, some of the hollowness melted away.

The idea of rescuing Smudge merged into an image of her mad dash out of the house next door with the cat in her arms which, in turn, brought a picture of the open patio door into sharp focus. She knew she should go shut it, but for some reason, the darkened back of the bungalows seemed more menacing than the lighted front walk. Maybe shadows and hiding places provided by large trees and bushes caused the difference in atmospheres.

At the very least, Beryl decided she should check to see that Joey had closed up the house. The night would be cold. If the door were left open, the furnace would turn on and run all night. Not only that, but a stray dog or cat might get into the house … or a racoon. Wild animals could cause a lot of damage. "Fine time to think of that, missy," Beryl scolded herself aloud. The sound of her voice woke the cat who yawned widely as he stretched his length across her lap to dig his claws into the arm of the chair.

"Hey," Beryl flicked a finger at his paws. "None of that." The move surprised Smudge into jumping down and heading toward the kitchen. His bed and litter box were set up in the laundry room, the same location he'd been used to next door, except for his food. Beryl made a mental note to speak to Joey soon about constructing a stair-step platform similar to the one George had built next to their clothes washer. The shelf not only would allow her to raise his kibbles and water away from the commode, but also make it easier for her to reach the bowls without having to double over. She was in reasonably good shape for her age, but as the years sped away, she found straightening up was becoming increasingly more difficult.

Beryl knew she was procrastinating and took a few deep breaths as she pondered again going back to Hazel's house. She also realized she was hesitating because of the unknown person she'd heard walking overhead. Was her earlier belief that the person wasn't a threat due to a false sense of security in Jessica's presence? *What are the chances, really, that whoever was sneaking around had been the arsonist?*

Now, in the safety and comfort of her living room, she wondered if the person she'd heard when she was in the crawl space might have frightened her more than she cared to admit. *Why hadn't she called out to see if it had been Joey or even Doe or Kelsey?* She then reversed her thought. *If they had a right to be in the house, why had they run when they heard her scream?* She strained to focus on what she'd heard … the footsteps definitely had been running away. As hard as she tried, though, Beryl couldn't figure out the direction of the retreat. She had no idea if the person had fled the house or hidden in another room. Building up her courage to check on the house next door, Beryl thought of another possibility. *Even if the person had run out of the house, he or she might have returned since.*

The mental picture of a criminal breaking into Hazel's house made Beryl think of Butch. She knew he would have a good laugh over her letting her imagination run so wild. Her guilt over leaving the house open overcame her fictional confrontation with a prowler, and she rose to fetch her sweater jacket. All she had to do, really, was go to the patio next door and check to see if the door was open. If it was, she simply had to slide it shut.

While she stood between the coat closet and her front door as she buttoned the jacket, Beryl thought of Jessica and considered asking for her company on the mission. *Ridiculous*, Beryl thought as she again envisioned the laugh Butch would have at her expense … because of course, the word would spread throughout the fire house and on to the police station.

I'm being silly. I'm not so old that I have to rely on someone to assist me, she mentally chastised herself. *Besides,* she added to further bolster her courage, *nothing bad has ever happened in this community.*

Each evening as darkness fell, Beryl would close the drapes and turn on the outside lights, front and back. Before peeking out the back door this night, she switched off the living room lamp and killed the patio lights. If anyone happened to be hanging around behind the bungalows, she didn't want to be seen or silhouetted in the door as she went out. "Too much TV," she whispered to herself, as she swallowed a nervous chuckle. She didn't, however, turn the lights back on as she approached the glass and pushed aside the curtain just enough to slide open the door and slip out. Quietly, she reclosed the panel and stood with her back against it until her eyes adjusted to the darkness.

Lights blazed in the courtyard of the Big House, but their brilliance didn't penetrate more than halfway across the lawn. Beryl focused on the shadow cast by the large spruce between her and the Bennets' backyard as she cautiously headed next door. No lights were on in or outside the house, so Beryl was only a few feet from the building before she saw the slider was closed and the drapes had been drawn.

She felt a cold shiver run down her spine, as if a drop of ice water had just trickled down her back. At the same moment, she felt a wave of relief that she needn't go any closer to the house. She didn't bother to wait or wonder who might have come and gone, or if they might still be inside. With an abrupt about-face, she scurried back to her own door, thrust it aside and leapt into the living room. Untangling herself from the curtain, she managed to close and lock the door before she fell into the nearest chair, took a deep breath and let it out slowly. *Of course, you nitwit*, she convinced herself, eventually. *Joey came back and closed up.* She'd check with him in the morning, but that had to be what happened. She needn't have worried. Joey was a dependable young man.

She was startled out of her thoughts when the cat rubbed himself against her leg before sauntering off toward the lighted kitchen. He stopped to glance at her only when he'd reached the corner of the counter. Glad for the distraction, Beryl dutifully followed the cat to discover an empty food bowl that she picked up and put into the dishwasher. One change she'd made to Hazel's arrangement was to put Smudge's food and water on a mat in the kitchen. Beryl didn't think they belonged in his bathroom, at least not until they could be set up and out of the way of the kitty commode.

"No more to eat for you, young man. Time for bed," she admonished as she headed for the garage. She needed a box for his bed, at least temporarily. She'd visit the local pet store in the morning to get more cat essentials, including a bed and a scratching post, but for tonight, she'd layer some old towels in a cardboard box.

After finding what she was looking for, she stopped to examine the coat still on the hanger she'd hooked over the knob of a cupboard. She studied it for a moment and wondered about its history and previous owner before she retreated into the house.

In the laundry room, she prepared the cat's bed, a task that Smudge watched with all the curiosity for which felines are accused. Beryl then shut him into the room. She wanted to get to know his habits and for him to get to know the house before she let him roam about at night.

In her own bedroom, she fell into a heavy sleep soon after burrowing beneath the green quilt. Too quickly, it seemed, she struggled into wakefulness from a dream in which she was slogging through a field of flowers as tall as cornstalks. She felt as if she were suffocating in thickly perfumed air. The scent seemed still to be in her nostrils and throat as her eyes fluttered open. She didn't start awake, but merely rose into full consciousness, curled on her right side with her back to the door into the living room. The illuminated display of her bedside clock read 2:07. She was suddenly certain something had roused her, but she didn't know what it had been. She lay quiet and listened, the flowery scent of her dream still in her nose.

Unless she had overnight company on the sofa, Beryl left the bedroom door open. She considered turning over to look into the other room, but her instinct told her to remain still. She was about to close her eyes, the better to hear, when she saw a pinpoint of light touch the top of the dresser three feet in front of her face. As she watched, frozen with fright, the beam moved along the wall and hovered on the closet door beyond the bureau.

As her eyes followed the light, Beryl sensed movement in the room. Someone was behind her. She felt a chill creep up her spine. Her skin tingled with sudden cold. Who was in her room? How had they gotten into the house?

Slowly, very slowly, so as to make neither sound nor motion that would draw the intruder's attention,

Beryl slid her left hand beneath the pillow. She was ready to move quickly if she had to, but at the moment, she took her time. After what seemed like an hour but was probably less than half a minute, her fingers touched the spare remote control to her car. Moving no more than the pressure required by her index finger, she pressed the panic button. Suddenly, the car horn's staccato beep sounded from behind the wall, alternating with a louder blast.

"Whaaa . . ." The sudden cacophony surprised the exclamation from the prowler's throat.

Beryl didn't move until she heard the intruder's footsteps leave the bedroom. As she turned to try to catch a glimpse of the person, she heard a thud, followed by a crash and a low curse. She imagined the prowler stumbling into a chair. Seconds later, Beryl heard the front door slam. Weak with fright, she fumbled the phone off the night stand and, with shaking fingers, pressed 9 1 1.

Chapter 11

Nadine woke at 5:17 Saturday morning. Something had caused her eyes to pop open, but she didn't know what, so she lay still, listening for sounds. After several minutes, when she'd heard nothing that she thought might have awakened her, she closed her eyes. She was certain whatever noise had roused her had come from outside. It made perfect sense. She loved a cool bedroom and usually cracked her window at night.

A neighborhood dog, she thought and burrowed down into the warmth of her down comforter, hoping to drift back into the half-sleep from which she'd stirred. She concentrated on relaxing her body, beginning with her toes, feet and ankles. When she reached her face and neck without the slightest feeling of returning drowsiness, she knew it was useless. Silently, she began to count backwards from 100. Reaching 32, still without a hint of sleepiness, she opened her eyes in frustration and got out of bed, wrapped her blue fleece robe around herself and padded to the kitchen in fuzzy pink slippers. "Might as well make coffee," she muttered into the predawn silence.

Ten minutes later, she took her steaming mug of coffee onto the balcony. If she couldn't sleep, she might as well watch the sun rise, she'd decided. Her apartment was on the west side of the Big House, so her early morning view would be the mountains slowly lighting up from the highest peaks down to the foothills. The scene was ever-changing, and one of which she never tired. Smiling to herself at the perfect grammar of her thought, she looked toward Beryl's backyard and almost dropped her coffee.

Setting the cup on the patio table and rushing into the condo, she raced to the kitchen to grab the phone. As she hurried back to the balcony, she picked up the camera that she'd left on the side table after removing it from the tripod the evening before. With her elbows on the railing to steady the heavy equipment, she first focused the viewfinder on the house next door to Beryl's. Smoke was seeping out of the window only a few yards from Beryl's home.

Snapping off a few pictures before she straightened to phone in the emergency, Nadine saw a blur of motion between the two houses. *Was that a person running along the street? Had he seen the smoke? Was he going for help?*

She swiveled the camera to the eastern side of the Bennets' bungalow, her finger remaining on the shutter release. Several frames later, between the Bennet house and the one farther to the east, she caught sight of a car moving in the direction of the main road. Her view of the rest of Sunnyvale's southern border stopped at the midpoint of that cottage, blocked by the wall of the Big House.

Without wasting time on frustration, wishes and regrets, she set the camera on the table with her coffee mug, picked up the cordless and dialed 9 1 1.

Speaking clearly and trying to remain calm, she gave the dispatcher what scant information she could. She'd not quite finished when the emergency operator informed her that they'd already received a call for the address and the fire department was on its way. With a quick "thank you," Nadine ended the call and immediately punched in Beryl's number.

"Come on, come on," she muttered, staring intently at Beryl's cottage as if her stare could wake the woman and bring her to the phone faster. While Nadine waited, she watched a man come into view. He was walking rapidly behind the Bennets' house toward Beryl's. At almost the same instant, another man appeared in the alley between the two bungalows. The alley man must have seen the walking man because he rushed toward the hurrying figure, pointing backward toward the window where smoke was now oozing more heavily.

"Ungh" was Beryl's unintelligible greeting, pulling Nadine's attention to the phone at her ear.

"Beryl, wake up," she nearly shouted into the mouthpiece. "Hazel's house is burning. Yours could catch. You've got to get out."

"Huh," Beryl sounded only slightly more alert this time. Still sounding groggy, she slurred out the words, "I'm awake. I'm awake." With every word, she did sound more aware until, finally, she asked in a nearly clear-headed voice, "A fire?"

"Next door. Hazel's house. Smoke is pouring out of the windows," Nadine exaggerated, hoping to instill a little urgency into her friend. "The fire department is on its way, but you must get out. Your houses are so close, the fire could jump to your place."

"Okay, I'm up. Gotta get some clothes on, though."

"Me, too," Nadine said. "Then I'm coming over."

Minutes later, dressed in a pair of slacks and a heavy sweater, Nadine left the Big House and hurried across the lawn. By that time, others had begun to gather across the lawn. A young man was holding his arms wide, obviously trying to keep people from getting too close to the burning building. Nadine recognized him as Joey Marconi, Sunnyvale's exercise instructor and part-time handyman. She realized he'd been the man who'd rushed into her view while she waited for Beryl to answer the phone, the "walking man." Beside Joey, she caught sight of Henry helping Joey to herd back the onlookers. She now knew Henry had been the man who'd come from between the two houses, her "alley man."

Nadine skirted around behind the growing crowd, looking for her friend. With a feeling of relief, she spotted Beryl on the far edge of the throng, ignoring Henry's attempt to have her move back. Nadine realized with some surprise that Beryl was talking to Jessica. As Nadine rushed up to the two women, she saw they were watching a firefighter as he set a ladder against Hazel's house and began to climb rapidly.

"What's he doing up there?" Nadine asked, nearly out of breath from her dash to find Beryl. "Why isn't he going into the house?"

"The first thing we do is cut a hole in the roof," Jessica said, turning to nod briefly at Nadine. The young woman was not in uniform, but wore navy blue sweats. She looked as if she'd been out for a run with her dark hair pulled back in a ponytail and a sweat band around her head. Having acknowledged Nadine, she turned back to the action while she explained further. "It creates a chimney effect. Pulls the gases and smoke up and relieves the pressure inside the house. There's less chance of flashover or backdraft."

Standing between the other two women, Nadine took another minute to catch her breath. She couldn't see the emergency vehicles from where she stood, but the early morning was alight with strobing blue and red bouncing off buildings, bushes and trees.

"What's flashover?" she asked, once her breathing was under control.

"Basically, it's when everything in a room ignites because of the extreme heat," Jessica said. "When objects get hot enough, they emit gases; and when all that gas suddenly ignites, it causes flashover."

"They're both explosions, right … flashover and backdraft?" Beryl commented. When Jessica nodded, Beryl said, "So what's the difference?"

"Backdraft is air driven while flashover is the result of extreme heat." Jessica explained.

"Oh," Nadine remarked, not sure if she understood the whole concept. "How bad is this fire, do you think?" she said instead of asking for any further clarification.

Before Jessica could reply, their attention was drawn back to the fire as smoked poured upward out of the hole in the roof, and two more firefighters appeared in the alleyway between the cottages. Hauling a large hose, they reached the window just as the man on the ladder grabbed the side rails, jumped off the rung and slid to the ground. The descent was quick and looked as efficient as a dance step. As soon as the first fireman removed the ladder, the others proceeded to break the window and send a forceful blast of water into the room.

At that moment, Beryl uttered a low groan. "Any of her personal belongings that escaped the fire will be totally ruined now. I hope there was nothing Doe wanted to keep."

They watched in silence for several more minutes before the water was turned off and yet another fireman poked his head out of the hole where the window had been and spoke to his buddies.

"Looks like everything's under control," Jessica remarked and waved as the man in the window caught sight of her.

"Nice looking guys," Beryl teased Jessica. Nadine suspected her friend was trying to relieve the tension they must be feeling as much as she herself.

The younger woman rolled her eyes. "Yes, and don't they just know it."

"They certainly made a presence in the grocery store when I was shopping a few days ago," Nadine said, happy to add to the distraction. "Strolled through the produce department, larger than life. They seemed so big, like football players."

"That's only because you're short," Beryl joked, wrinkling her nose at Nadine.

Jessica chuckled and answered in agreement with Nadine. "They do enjoy strutting their stuff. I'm willing to bet there were at least four of them and no one was pushing a cart. Right?"

Nadine sputtered a laugh. "Now that you mention it …"

"Looks like the crowd is breaking up," Jessica said abruptly, pointing behind Nadine with her chin.

Nadine turned to see people losing interest and beginning to walk away, some to nearby cottages while most headed back to the Big House. Too late to avoid his glance, she saw Henry staring at her. "Drat," she muttered as he elbowed his way through a cluster of men and women to approach her. She didn't want to listen to his opinions on the fire and the efforts of the firefighters, but realized she couldn't avoid a confrontation. As he drew closer, she formed her lips into a smile.

"Good morning, ladies." He greeted the three women with more heartiness than the occasion warranted, Nadine thought. "Some fire, hey?" he added rhetorically.

"You must have been one of the first to get here," Jessica said. "Were you the one who phoned it in?"

"Not me," Henry said.

Not I, Nadine corrected silently.

Fortunately, Henry wasn't able to read her thoughts as he went on speaking. "I caught the call on my scanner. When I realized the address was Sunnydale, I got up and came out to see. Just like everyone else," he added. He jerked his head to indicate over his shoulder. "Joey got here about the same time I did. I don't know what he's doing here so early, but maybe he's the one who reported it." Henry looked the picture of innocence with widened eyes.

"Jessica Westin?" A deep male voice drew

everyone's attention to the area between the two houses. A police officer was approaching from the street while another stopped at the end of the alleyway.

The young woman stepped forward to acknowledge herself. "Yes?" She didn't appear surprised or alarmed to be hailed by a couple of uniforms.

"Will you come with me, miss?" the officer extended an arm toward where his partner stood.

"Sure." Jessica turned to catch Nadine's eye. "Call you later," she said.

They'd had a good reunion, but decided they had much more to talk about since they'd parted as teacher and student almost 15 years ago, so Nadine and Jessica planned to meet again that afternoon or evening, depending on Jessica's schedule.

"Hen-REE." The shrill cry came from the direction of the Big House as Jessica disappeared with the two officers. Along with Beryl and Henry, Nadine spun toward the urgency of the sound to see Clara hobbling toward them in feathery slippers and what looked like a flowing silk kimono beneath her calf-length mink coat. She had apparently taken time to apply makeup and fix her hair, so one would think she also could have put on clothes more suitable for the chilly September morning.

She was obviously too late to watch the fire, Nadine thought, so why was she rushing toward them? Henry looked as if he'd wanted to follow Jessica and the policemen out to the street, but Clara was nearly upon him. At the last moment, she slipped in her two-inch heels and fell against his arm, grabbing on and holding tight. Glancing over at the Big House, Nadine saw Clara's "ladies in waiting" had stopped at the edge of the courtyard, not venturing onto the grass. Rather, they stood with several other residents and kept an anxious eye on their elderly patron. Nadine spotted other Sunnydale residents ogling from their balconies.

"Henry looks like he wants to talk to you," Beryl said quietly into Nadine's ear. Her tone held a note of amusement. All humor was gone from her next words, though. "When you're done here, come have coffee with me. I've stuff to tell you."

Nadine spun with concern. Beryl had sounded dead serious, but she was already out of normal-voice ear shot. Nadine was about to follow when she heard Clara speak to Henry. As with most hard-of-hearing people, the nonagenarian spoke louder than necessary, so Nadine couldn't help but overhear. "What's happened to Hazel's house? First your good friend George dies, then his wife. Now someone's trying to burn down their house. What is going on here, Henry?"

Nadine slowed her pace to hear if Henry would reply, but all she could make out was a low growl. She also wanted to know what was going on with all the misfortune that had befallen the Bennets so recently. Henry had been first at the fire. What had he been doing so early in the morning. Nadine doubted he could have dressed and gotten to the house so quickly if he hadn't awakened until the scanner announced the fire at Sunnydale. Her thought turned to Mabel's comment, and Nadine wondered again if Henry could he have been on his way to visit Hazel and not Beryl when Mabel spotted him crossing the lawn? If so, why so late at night?

Nadine put her concerns about Henry on hold as she reached Beryl's patio and approached her friend. "What do you have to tell me?"

"In a minute," Beryl said. She had stopped at the double glass doors, one hand on the latch. Her head was tilted as if she were deep in thought. "I want to check something." With a sudden beckoning of her hand, she indicated Nadine should follow her.

Entering the house, Nadine stayed close behind Beryl as she went directly to the front door and out onto the stoop. Outside, Nadine swung her gaze in the direction Beryl nodded, just in time to see a police woman put her hand on the top of Jessica's head as the young firefighter lowered herself into the back of a patrol car.

"What are they doing?" Nadine felt confused and frantic as understanding dawned. "Is she being arrested?"

"Don't know," Beryl said in a lower and more controlled voice, "but it's what I suspected was going on."

Chapter 12

As Beryl watched the police car drive away with Jessica in the back seat, the activities of the previous day and the interrupted sleep, followed by the excitement of the fire next door, were suddenly weighing on her, but she doubted she'd be able to sleep anytime soon. She felt as though there was something she should be doing, but she couldn't think of what or why. Her mind seemed to have shut down. Her body tingled with restlessness even as her limbs felt heavy and useless. A howling screech from somewhere inside the house roused her from the stupor.

"What in the world …" Nadine cried, pressing her fingers to her ears.

"Smudge." Beryl threw the name over her shoulder as she rushed indoors. She hurried to the far end of the kitchen and yanked open the door to the laundry room. The yowling stopped abruptly. Out of the utility area stomped a black cat who gave Beryl one haughty glare as he headed for the mat that Beryl had placed on the floor for his food and water bowls.

"Oops." Beryl sputtered a laugh. "Sorry, your royal highness. I'll have your breakfast ready in a flash."

"When did you get a cat?" Nadine asked, sinking

onto one of the low chairs at the counter. She stared at the feline and seemed totally amazed that Beryl could have acquired a house pet within the last 12 hours. In a quiet voice, as if thinking aloud, she said, "Where did you get her?"

"Him," Beryl corrected without looking up from her chore. She pulled the tab on a small can of cat food and upended the contents onto a saucer. She couldn't blame Nadine for her surprise or questions. Considering all that had happened in a day and a half, Beryl could hardly take in Smudge's presence herself, particularly since he seemed to have taken over her house and her life quite boldly in a very short time indeed. She set the dish on the mat and barely had time to remove her hand when the cat dug in. After refreshing the water in his bowl, she crossed the room to sit at the counter beside Nadine. "He's Hazel's cat. That's Smudge."

"Ahhh." Comprehension dawned and cleared the frown lines from Nadine's forehead. "Doe's note. This is the Smudge you were to keep a lookout for." When Beryl merely nodded but said nothing further, Nadine prompted, "Did he come knocking on your door?"

The muzzy feeling had returned, causing Beryl to stop and think about the question while ignoring the sarcasm. The distraction of releasing and then feeding the cat had lifted some of the fog from Beryl's brain temporarily, but the process of mentally shifting through images of the previous night seemed to require great effort. Bringing back the evening's events when she'd gone hunting for Smudge, Beryl remembered the stranger she'd heard in Hazel's living room. In an instant, another, more frightening memory overshadowed every other thought. She reached out and grabbed Nadine' forearm. "Someone was in my house last night."

"What," Nadine gasped. Her glance ran over Beryl's face and neck. "My lord. What happened? Who was it? They didn't attack you, did they?"

"No," Beryl assured her friend. Before she could explain, Nadine pressed on.

"You didn't attack them, did you?"

Beryl gave a hearty laugh at the idea. "I might have a few years ago or so," she admitted, "but I'm a little wiser and less agile these days." Speaking of the episode helped to relieve some of the panic. Since the incident was several hours past and her fright abated somewhat, she could find humor in Nadine's assumption that Beryl would take the offensive in a threatening situation, however tongue-in-cheek the remark may have been uttered.

"Tell me what happened," Nadine had regained enough control to sound impatient "Who was it? What did he want?" she asked. The frown lines were back.

Beryl took a deep breath, wondering why her statement hadn't been perfectly clear to Nadine. "I don't know who it was, and I have no idea what he wanted. As far as I can tell, he did nothing except upend the table lamp and knock over George and Hazel's picture frame. Nothing broke, thank goodness, but he made such a racket, I figured for sure he'd broken the side table and smashed the light. As to what happened, well it's just what I said … someone came into my house while I was asleep.

Whoever it was must have made some sort of noise or maybe I sensed their presence because it brought me out of the crazy dream I was having."

"I thought Sunnydale was a safe place to live," Nadine declared, a note of anger creeping into her voice. "First, someone sets fire to the house next door and now you tell me your home has been invaded, and all in a single night." She suddenly clapped a hand over her mouth. Removing it almost immediately, she said, "Do you suppose it's the same person? Could he have broken in to *your* house to start a fire?"

Beryl stared at her friend for almost half a minute as the idea took some time to penetrate the haze building in her head again. Finally, she said, "Don't be absurd. Never occurred to me. He's been burning *empty* houses." She paused for a minute to wonder if Nadine might be right. Was the arsonist taking his vandalism to another level? Even in her numb state, Beryl refused to consider the idea seriously. Murderers might set fires to destroy evidence, but arsonists didn't intentionally kill people.

"So, who do you think broke in … and why?" Nadine repeated her earlier question, fortunately breaking Beryl's train of thought.

The question prompted Beryl to concentrate on the sharpest memory of the previous night. She began to recall some of her feelings. "I'm pretty sure I smelled perfume." At the quizzical look on Nadine's face, Beryl explained, "My dream … in my dream, I was suffocating in a field of very tall flowers." Her eyes widened with new understanding as she shifted in her seat to face Nadine directly. "I bet it wasn't a *he* who was in my house. It was a *she*, and the smell of her perfume woke me." Beryl paused to reflect, then proceeded to describe in more detail what she remembered about the dream and about coming awake to realize someone was in her bedroom. The retelling brought back the anxiety she'd experienced and her heartbeat quicken.

Nadine was spellbound, hanging on Beryl's every word. "Weren't you frightened to death?"

"Of course, I was," Beryl snapped the reply. Her exhaustion, coupled with the returning unease, made her peevish. She inhaled deeply and slowly let out her breath.

"What did you do?" Nadine seemed oblivious of Beryl's irritation.

Beryl took another steadying breath before explaining about the key fob she kept beneath her pillow.

"You set off your car's alarm system," Nadine exclaimed. "That's brilliant." She clapped her hands in delight before instantly sobering. "Tell me you phoned the police."

"I certainly did," Beryl reassured her friend, adding with some pride. "They arrived in no time. I barely had a chance to put on my robe before two officers were at my door."

"Did they catch the guy?" Nadine's face lit up in anticipation of a positive outcome. Obviously, she'd forgotten Beryl's theory about the gender.

Beryl shook her head. "'Fraid not. They didn't see anyone in the neighborhood on their way here. Once I told them what'd happened, the first thing they did was search the house to make sure the person was gone. That's when I noticed the table was askew and the picture frame on its face. The lamp had fallen behind the wingback. I filled the cops in a little more, and they went out to search around the house. Said they didn't see anyone so figured he was long gone and probably wouldn't be back." Beryl paused briefly before recalling, "I didn't think at the time, it must have been a woman because of the perfume."

"Should you call the police and let them know?" Nadine asked.

Beryl considered, then said, "Man or woman, the officers said they didn't see anyone, so I guess it doesn't really matter now." After another brief pause, she shrugged and continued with her story. "Their theory was that the intruder probably mistook my house for the one next door, thinking they were entering an empty home." She rubbed her hands over her face in an attempt to relieve some of her exhaustion. "The cops were here until nearly four this morning."

Nadine gently put a hand on Beryl's forearm, clearly upset. "And I woke you not long after that. You must not have gotten much sleep at all."

Beryl managed a weak smile and a shake of her head. "'S true I'd barely gotten back to bed, but you were right to call. My house didn't catch fire, but it might have. Besides, I'd have hated to miss the excitement." This last was said with a return of her good humor, despite the fatigue.

At that moment, their conversation was interrupted by Smudge who sauntered over to rub against Beryl's leg. He'd finished his post-meal grooming and seemed to want attention. His presence brought Beryl's other adventure to mind, and she was trying to figure out how to begin when Nadine spoke.

"Where did you find Smudge? Was he outside? Is that why Doe couldn't find him?"

Nadine's questions were the perfect opening, as if she'd read Beryl's mind. "Funny you should ask," Beryl began, then paused. She wondered how Nadine would react to the news of another prowler. Too coincidental? Beryl suddenly speculated on the chance that not just two, but three separate individuals would have invaded the two houses on the same evening, a few hours apart ... the person creeping through the living room, the midnight stalker and whoever set the fire. *Or*, she thought, *all the same*?

Uncertain how to voice the confusing idea, Beryl stalled for time. She hoisted the cat onto her lap and stroked his fur as she began to speak slowly, carefully choosing words as her mind played over images. She first explained her concern for the cat which led to her investigation of the house next door. She emphasized that she'd really only meant to play her flashlight through the glass when she described how she found the panel unlocked and assumed that Joey hadn't returned to close up. As she spoke of her decision to search the basement, part of her mind strayed to the probability of one person moving back and forth between both homes and the possible motive for such actions.

Had the creeper left Hazel's and gone to hide in Beryl's house while Beryl was still in the cellar? She froze, speechless at the thought that someone had been in her house while she had been unaware of the presence, even as she went to bed. She imagined a black-clad form gaining access through her own patio doors that she'd left unlocked when she'd gone to look for Smudge. Had they stowed away in her bedroom closet? Were they in her room all the while and woke her by fiddling with the louvered doors? With a mental shake of her head, she reminded herself that her midnight guest had been a woman wearing cloying perfume. Beryl was certain the scent would have exposed the woman if she'd been in the house before Beryl went to bed. If Hazel's intruder had been the same woman, would Beryl have smelled the perfume or had she bolted too fast from the house?

"Another break-in?" Nadine's shrill question shattered Beryl's unwelcome imaginings and snapped her back to the realization that she'd just described the footsteps she'd heard in Hazel's house.

"I don't know." To her surprise, the words sounded fairly calm when she really wanted to wail with frustration. Feeling her agitation grow, she deflected the question, "I *wish* I could remember if I closed that patio door or left it open when I entered Hazel's house. If it was open, someone might have been curious enough to come inside and poke around." At Nadine's skeptical look, Beryl felt her defenses rise. "Someone from the Big House or one of the bungalow residents, taking an evening walk, could have come by and wondered why the door was open. That would mean the intrusion had been innocent and I simply scared the person into running." She looked hopefully at Nadine, wanting to see verification in her friend's face that the incident was as innocent as a curiosity-seeker or good Samaritan being frightened away when Beryl had shrieked.

Nadine didn't seem quite as accepting of the benign solution. "Surely, they'd have called out to announce their presence if they weren't up to mischief. I certainly would," she declared in a no-nonsense tone.

Beryl shrugged. "Maybe. If they were feeling guilty or skittish about being where they shouldn't, maybe not. Remember, Hazel died just the night before. If the person knew that, maybe they thought a scream coming from beneath the floor was her ghost." Beryl raised her eyebrows at Nadine, hoping her fanciful speculation might ease some of the tension that had built up between them. Beryl couldn't explain why, but she was embarrassed to admit to a friend who credited her with exaggerated detecting skills that she had no idea in which direction the person had fled. Had they escaped through the patio door as Beryl herself had done?

Nadine swallowed hard, looking both terrified and distraught. Her eyes widened when she asked, "Do you think you let the arsonist into the house?"

The thought straightened Beryl's spine with a jerk. The quick move propelled Smudge from her lap and onto the floor where he scrabbled off toward the living room. Only half conscious of the feline's flight, she stared at Nadine as her mind rejected the possibility and she tried to convince herself that an innocent person had entered the house. She was exhausted and finding it increasingly difficult to think. She needed sleep. Finally, with a shrug, she said, "I gotta talk to Joey."

Silence fell on the room for nearly a minute before Nadine asked in a subdued voice, "Why do you think the police arrested Jessica?"

Beryl's mind had shut down. She briefly squeezed her eyes shut, hoping to focus on something other than her possible culpability in a crime. "They probably just wanted to talk to her, get her opinion on the fire. She was one of the first to arrive, wasn't she?"

"I don't know," Nadine replied. "I saw two men running around the house, but then I had to phone the emergency line and call you. After that, I went inside to get dressed. By the time I joined you and Jessica on your patio, there was quite a crowd milling about. I have no idea when, in all that confusion, Jessica got there."

Beryl fought to think clearly. "I'll call Butch. He can find out what's going on." When Beryl didn't move to make the call, Nadine stood.

"You look like you're about to fall off that chair," she said. "I'll leave so you can go to bed."

Beryl pushed herself out of her seat. "You're right," was all she could manage to say as she walked Nadine to the patio door and slide it aside.

Stepping onto the flagstone patio, Nadine stopped and turned back, looking perplexed. "I thought you said the Bennets kept pretty much to themselves."

"They did," Beryl said. "What makes you ask?"

Nadine shrugged. "I overheard Clara refer to George Bennet as Henry's good friend. Looking at their house, so close to yours, I'm remembering what

Mabel said about seeing Henry headed this way. I wonder if he might have been coming to visit Hazel. That would be strange, though, wouldn't it?"

"What do you mean?" Beryl's head was beginning to ache, trying to follow Nadine's logic.

"Well," Nadine went on, "Mabel said she saw him last week. He was hurrying across the lawn, late at night. Late enough that she fancied a tryst between the two of you. George was dead and buried. Either Doe or Kelsey or both were here taking care of Hazel, but neither one would have let anyone in to see her, according to what you've told me. So what could Henry have been up to? Do you think he might have been visiting Doe or Kelsey?"

Beryl stared. She couldn't seem to wrap her mind around the complexity of the associations, never mind give Nadine an answer as to Henry's actions or motive. She really needed to sleep.

Chapter 13

Beryl awoke shortly before 2:00 Saturday afternoon. Feeling more tired than refreshed, she lay still while her mind woke up. When she remembered the intruder in her room, she felt her skin prickle as if a ghost presence remained. Had it been the arsonist? No. She rejected the thought. The local firebug entered empty houses, and she refused to believe the person had mistaken her house for Hazel's vacant one. Besides, she was pretty sure arsonists were usually male and she was fairly certain the person in her bedroom had been female.

Who had been in Hazel's house last night? Was it the arsonist or the bedroom invader? And who started the fire? Are we looking at one person? Two? Three? As she tried to work out how many strangers were wandering the neighborhood, Beryl's head began to pound.

Tossing aside the quilt, she swung her legs over the side of the bed and searched with her toes for her slippers. Smudge, curled up on the bottom of the quilt, opened an eye and stretched languidly as Beryl rose and headed for the bathroom. She showered away most of her remaining grogginess and thoughts of the previous night. Pulling on woolen slacks and a comfortable cotton-blend tunic, she strode into the kitchen, leaving the cat to return to his nap. She needed coffee to banish the lingering fuzziness from her brain. Perhaps then she could think more clearly.

After downing the first half cup, she remembered she was supposed to phone Butch for some reason. It took another jolt of caffeine for her to recall why. She was looking at the phone, sipping her second full cup and envisioning dialing when the cordless rang, startling her into slopping hot liquid onto her chin.

"Shoot," she gasped, mopping her face with one hand while lifting the phone with the other.

"Rather you didn't," came the deep rumble of a voice into her ear.

"Didn't what?" Beryl snapped. She was too distracted to appreciate Butch's humor as she dabbed at her skin.

"Shoot," he said with a definite smile in his tone. "I'd rather you didn't shoot."

"You made me burn myself. I'm in no mood for jokes," she replied with irritation. "What do you want."

"Nice way to greet an old friend who's only concerned for your safety and well-being," he said. "Shall I hang up and try again another day?"

Beryl took a deep breath and let it out slowly. "Please don't. Actually, I was about to call you."

"Oh?" Butch queried.

"You first," Beryl insisted. "To what do I owe the honor of this call." She was beginning to feel better. This simple connection to her old friend lifted her spirits immediately.

"My department snitch tells me you had an unexpected visitor in the wee hours of the morning," he said, referring tongue-in-cheek to the last partner with whom he'd worked before retiring and who kept Butch informed of minor police matters he thought might be of interest to the ex-detective. "What's going on down there in the little big city?" Butch asked.

Beryl smiled at the description. Since he'd moved to a small mountain town, Butch referred to Denver as the "big city" and to Arvada as the "little big city." Mulling over his question, she sobered. "I honestly don't know, Butch. A bunch of weird things happened last night and I'm just getting awake enough to try to sort through them."

"Like what?" he asked. All playfulness gone from his voice. "Talk to me."

Thinking back to the previous evening, Beryl said, "I guess I should begin when I went next door to check on the cat." She proceeded to tell Butch about discovering the unlocked patio door which allowed her to enter Hazel's house to look for Smudge. The retired detective listened in silence until she ended with her unease over the police driving off with Jessica.

"That's why I was about to phone you," she said with sudden recollection. "Can you find out why they took her to the station and if she's been charged with anything?"

"As far as I know, the investigating team did interview a young woman this morning, but they're not holding anyone."

"You were going to tell me why you phoned," Beryl said, "and I'm the one doing all the talking."

"The snitch says there's been a few odd

occurrences in your neighborhood recently. Wanted to know if I'd heard anything from you, any rumors," Butch explained. "He's uneasy, particularly when that fire broke out next door to you so soon after your nine-one-one emergency on the midnight visitor. Figured I'd better find out what you've been up to. You know I promised Michael I'd look after you."

Beryl felt heat spread in her chest at the mention of Michael and the still-vivid memory of the friendship between the two men. Their bond had brought the two couples together. After Michael's fatal accident, the Yancys had been Beryl's lifeline to sanity. "Yes, and he made the same promise to you about Cicely and the kids, if I remember correctly." The lump in her throat prevented her from saying more.

After several seconds of silence, she heard Butch clear his throat before he spoke again. "There's something else you probably should know." She didn't care for the ominous tone to his voice, but she waited. Several heartbeats later, he said, "Your neighbor ... Hazel Bennet. Was that her name?" His question must have been rhetorical because he didn't wait for an answer. "My information is that she died of severe dehydration. Her doctor sees no reason for her condition and has requested an autopsy."

Beryl was speechless, taking in news that made no sense to her. Hazel hadn't looked well at George's funeral, and according to Doe, Hazel had suffered such severe eye pain that she'd had to lie in a darkened room, but that she had become so totally desiccated was incredible to Beryl. True, when she'd seen Hazel last week, she'd had that warm cloth covering her eyes, but she hadn't seemed at death's door. Not at all *Why hadn't Doe taken Hazel to the hospital, if she'd been that critical?*

"Beryl?" Butch's voice brought her back to the phone conversation. "Are you still there? Are you okay? Should I come down?"

"No," Beryl said quickly. Her mind was whirling over the shock of what she'd learned, and she realized she might have spoken too sharply to the bearer of the bad news. *Don't shoot the messenger*, she thought, regaining some control. "Sorry, Butch. Didn't mean to snap. What I mean is yes, I'm okay … or I will be … and no, you don't need to hold my hand. You are a dear friend, but there's really nothing you can do. I just need time to take it all in." Before he could protest, as she suspected he would, she said, "Look, I'll check with Cicely in a day or so and come for a visit."

After Butch reluctantly agreed to a delayed get-together, Beryl begged off and reiterated her promise to see him soon. She'd replaced the receiver and was pouring a fresh cup of coffee when the phone rang again.

"Who've you been talking to? Your line's been busy for hours," Nadine exaggerated, but continued before Beryl could think of an appropriate retort. "Jessica's here and wants to talk to both of us. She won't tell me what happened at her interrogation …"

"Interview" Beryl heard a voice in the background.

"… her *interview*," Nadine corrected as Beryl listened and grinned. She knew full well the importance law enforcement personnel placed on the difference between an interview and an interrogation. "As I was saying," Nadine continued, "Jessica refuses to tell me anything until you get here. Says she doesn't want to have to repeat herself, and she has questions for both of us, so please come up here to my place as soon as you can." There was a brief pause before Nadine repeated, "*Please.*"

Thankful for the distraction and finally able to get a word in, Beryl took a slow sip of coffee as she decided not to pass along the devastating news about Hazel until she'd had time to consider it herself. She swallowed, nodding into the receiver, then said with more than a hint of sarcasm, "Yes, I'm up. You didn't wake me this time. And I did get some much-needed sleep. Thanks for asking."

After a short pause, Nadine chuckled. "Sorry for my insensitivity in not first inquiring after your health. I'm very glad to hear you're well rested. Now, would you please get over here. I'm dying to hear what Jessica has to say."

Beryl snorted a laugh. "Of course, I will. I'm as curious as you are. If you'll get off the phone, I'll be on my way."

Nadine hung up.

Gazing out across the sunlit lawn toward the Big House, Beryl figured she wouldn't need anything but the long-sleeved tunic she was wearing with her blue slacks. Sliding into a pair of black leather brogues and deciding to carry her house key in her pants pocket instead of taking a purse, she stepped out onto the flagstones. Immediately, she heard hammering and hurried around the corner to find Joey on a painter's ladder. He'd apparently secured a plastic tarp over the hole in the roof and now he was sealing up Hazel's broken-out bedroom window with plywood.

"I need to talk to you," she said, walking over to look up at the handsome young man.

"Hi, Beryl." He beamed down at her. "I'm just finishing up here. Be with you in a sec."

After another couple of whacks to secure a nail or two, Joey leaned away from the house to examine his handiwork. "That should do it," he declared, jumping to the ground. He turned to face her as he folded the ladder. "What can I do you for?" he asked, favoring her with the gorgeous smile that creased his tanned cheeks. He didn't wait for her to speak, but slipped one arm between the middle rungs, balanced the ladder on his shoulder and headed toward the back of the house.

"When did you lock up yesterday," Beryl asked, turning to keep stride with him.

He stopped, looked toward the Big House, then back at her. "I didn't," he said in a low voice, although Beryl couldn't see anyone nearby who might overhear them.

"Why not?" she demanded, refusing to lower her voice. She couldn't believe what she was hearing. She'd always pegged Joey as conscientious and reliable.

Giving another nervous glance toward the main building, he leaned slightly toward her, his voice still barely above a whisper. "Because I wanted to look around."

"What?" Beryl bent backward to get a better look into his eyes. "What for?" she accused.

"You won't tell anyone, will you?" he asked.

Tell anyone that Sunnydale's handyman snooped through people's homes? Beryl wondered. Noncommittally, she said, "You know me."

Joey nodded, always ready to please the friend of a former police detective with contacts in the local department. He shrugged the ladder from his shoulder and set it on the ground, holding it upright. Keeping his voice low, he glanced around once more before saying, "The Bennets weren't who they pretended to be." Joey stared into her eyes as if trying to gauge her reaction.

Beryl stared back, frowning. *What was he talking about?* She didn't quite understand what she'd just heard and waited for him to explain.

He babbled on. "Since they're both dead and won't really care, I wanted to see if I could find anything that would tell me more about them." His expression soured. "Unfortunately, because of the fire, I didn't get to investigate this morning, like I'd planned. Now, whatever evidence I might have found has probably been destroyed." His eyes flashed with sudden excitement. "But maybe not. The fire was caught early, so there wasn't much damage." Again, his face fell. "Except for smoke and water."

Still dwelling on his declaration of the Bennets as being incredulous, she nearly laughed aloud. When she saw how serious and how transparent he was, she swallowed her initial response and, instead of chiding him, asked, "What makes you think the Bennets weren't who they said they were?"

"Henry Slater's said some things that've made me

wonder," Joey stated, as if that explained everything.

Beryl cocked her head and raised an eyebrow, waiting for Joey to go on. When he didn't, she prompted, "Like what?"

"I'm his personal trainer, you know," Joey said apropos to nothing, but with a flash of pride.

He's preening over the exclusivity of the position, Beryl realized. *That smugness sure isn't because Henry is any bigshot or has an amazing physique ... except maybe in the man's own head.* Aloud, she again prompted, "Go on."

"We talk." Joey raised a shoulder in a no-big-deal gesture as he continued. "I sort of told him I hope to be a detective someday."

Beryl swallowed her amusement over Joey's "sort of told him" and kept her face neutral. Now she was fairly certain Henry had been teasing Joey, planting seeds of doubt and intrigue. She didn't think kindly of Henry for picking on a gullible young man or on a recently deceased couple, and how absurd to think a couple as unassuming as the Bennets could be guilty of subterfuge. If George and Hazel had assumed different identities, how would Henry know? she concluded, satisfied her guess was correct that Henry was pulling Joey's leg.

"Well," the wannabe-detective leaned closer but forgot to keep his voice low in his excitement. "He said that there was a cold case right under my nose and I should suss it out. That was the word he used, *suss.* Had to look it up." Joey's cheeks reddened slightly at the admission.

The young man's piece of news was certainly interesting, but Beryl didn't have time to pry further information from him. At the moment, she had to get up to Nadine's condo and meet with Jessica. "Did he tell you the Bennets were involved in this cold case or simply held some sort of evidence?" she asked, taking a few more minutes to instill some questions in his mind ... questions he should get Henry to clarify. When Joey opened his mouth to speak again, she cut him off by asking, "Did you look around at all, last night?" The thought had struck her that he might have been the one she'd scared off with her scream. If so, she could cross one unknown off her mental list.

Joey shook his head. "Like I told you, I never got back here last night. That's why I'm afraid the fire might have destroyed anything I might have turned up."

"Did Henry tell you what to look for?" Even though she thought the older man was kidding with Joey, Beryl's curiosity had been piqued. *Why would Henry play such a trick? Was there a grain of truth behind his joke?* She didn't know Henry all that well, but she wouldn't have pegged him as the prankish type.

Joey shook his head again. "All he said was that the Bennets were involved in something that happened a long time ago, and that if I wanted to impress the police with my investigating skills, I should search their house for papers or pictures or proof of a crime."

Beryl thought for a minute, conscious of time passing and anxious to get to Nadine's, but wanting to know more. "I'm assuming the house has been released as a crime scene, seeing as you've been allowed to board up the window and patch the roof." At Joey's nod, she asked, "Are you thinking of going in to look around, even if any evidence might have been destroyed?"

He glanced nervously across the lawn. "Yeah, but later tonight. I don't want Mister P to catch me."

Visualizing Stan Pemberly who was Sunnydale's manager and Joey's boss, Beryl frowned. "Why so nervous? It's Saturday. Stan doesn't work weekends."

"Not usually, but with the fire and all, he came in today." The young handyman's eyes widened as if a terrible thought just struck him. "You won't tell him I left the place unlocked, will you?"

She wrinkled her nose and scowled at the implication that she'd snitch on him. "What do you think." She glanced at her watch. "I want to go in there with you, but right now, I've got something to do at the Big House." She looked toward the building for a second or two, then turned back to him. "I just might be able to get us both permission to be in the Bennets' house legitimately." She felt a shiver of excitement at the thought of returning to the place where she'd been so frightened the night before. "Meet me back here when you're off work for the day. Can you do that?"

"Yeah," Joey said, looking puzzled. "Sure. I guess so."

With that promise, Beryl turned and crossed the lawn to the Big House. As she headed for the elevators, she avoided eye contact with the few residents who were seated in comfortably stuffed chairs, arranged in conversation groups. She didn't want to get waylaid and lose more time gabbing. Her luck held when she found an empty car waiting on the ground floor, and she was able to get to Nadine's apartment without any further delay.

"About time," Nadine greeted her with a glower. She was standing in the open doorway of her condo when Beryl stepped off the elevator on the third floor. "I saw you chatting out there with Joey."

"Ahhh," Beryl retorted, striding into the condo, "just wait 'til you hear what we were talking about."

Chapter 14

"Whatever you and Joey talked about can wait," Nadine said as she closed the door behind Beryl and hurried back to the kitchen counter where, facing from the living room side, Jessica was partially hidden behind the open lid of a laptop. "If you'd wasted any more time, you'd've missed my pictures."

"It was important," Beryl protested, joining Nadine at the counter across from the young firefighter. "Hi, Jessica. What's going on?" As if she'd just realized what Nadine had said, Beryl looked from one woman to the other. "You're looking at pictures? I thought we were going to talk about Jessica's trip to the station."

"Be patient. You'll see in a minute. Jessica's loading my computer," Nadine explained, despite the fact that she had no idea what her former student was doing.

Jessica lifted her head for an instant, her eyes twinkling with merry fondness at Nadine before returning to her task. "I'm downloading the pictures Mrs. Rodd took from her balcony this morning."

"What pictures?" Beryl frowned at Nadine. "Don't tell me we're going to waste time on shots of a Colorado sunrise, lovely as they might be."

"The fire," Nadine said, staring intently at Jessica, as if that would speed up the process. "I got some photos of the fire and maybe the arsonist." In a much quieter voice, she added, "I hope."

"We had trouble finding the USB adapter for the camera's SD card, so you haven't missed anything yet," Jessica explained without looking up from the keyboard. "I'm just now copying the images to a folder on the desktop."

"Right," Beryl said, rolling her eyes to the ceiling. "I'm sure that makes sense to you, but I haven't a clue what you just said. Besides that, I haven't taken a picture in years. Now that they have these fancy-doodle things hooked to computers, I don't think I'll be turning into a photographer anytime soon. And don't get me started on people using their phones as cameras."

Nadine laughed along with Jessica over Beryl's self-deprecating grimace. "Roger taught me how to use his digital camera," Nadine informed her friend, "but he neglected to show me how he got the pictures into the computer so I could look at them or blow them up, if I want."

"Don't worry, Mrs. Rodd," Jessica briefly glanced up again. "I'll teach you sometime. Right now, the slide show is ready." She sat back on her stool and motioned the others to come around the counter.

"I keep telling you to call me Nadine," she scolded Jessica with a mock scowl. "I'm no longer your teacher and we're not in a classroom." She moved behind the young woman and stood beside Beryl. All eyes turned to the monitor as Jessica brought up the first image.

"Nice picture of my house," Beryl remarked, poking Nadine's arm with an elbow. "Have you been spying on me?"

"Hush," Nadine ordered, keeping her eyes on the screen. "There are more shots than just your place. You'll see."

Jessica scrolled slowly through the entire set of photos before selecting one to freeze on the screen.

"That's the one I was telling you about," Nadine said, feeling a twinge of excitement at the image of a person walking along the street between Beryl's and Hazel's cottages. The individual was wearing a hoodie, sweatpants and tennis shoes. "I was almost positive I saw someone there this morning." She put a hand on Jessica's shoulder and bent forward for a better view. "Pull up the next one. I focused on the other side of Hazel's house to see if the person would show up again, but all I remember seeing was a car. I don't know where the person went … if they got into the car or turned back toward Beryl's. Whatever the guy did, I missed 'em."

"Could've been a woman," Beryl observed.

"Maybe so," Nadine agreed.

Ignoring them, Jessica brought up the next three photos. The pictures were blurred, but she stopped each one on the screen and enlarged the area between Hazel's house and the neighbor to the east. The attempt didn't help the image. Nadine's photo was simply too blurry. The vehicle appeared to be white, moving toward the main street and finally disappearing from view as the frames progressed. Sunlight glare on the side window made the driver hard to distinguish. No person appeared on foot in any of the pictures, except for the single figure in the first shot. "That's it, ladies," Jessica said, swiveling around on the stool to face the other two.

Nadine felt a crush of disappointment. "I was hoping I'd taken a picture of the arsonist. If it was that person in the hoodie, I couldn't even tell for certain if it was a man or woman." She slid her eyes toward Beryl to acknowledge her friend's earlier observation. "I suppose whomever I captured along the street could have been a jogger who had seen smoke, called in the fire and left because he or she didn't want to get involved." She turned to Beryl for confirmation. "Witnesses do that, don't they? Refuse to come forward?"

"'Fraid so," Beryl agreed.

Thinking back to the morning, Nadine remembered the two figures who had appeared when she'd been waiting for Beryl to answer her phone. In a flash of excitement, she said, "We should ask Henry. He may have seen whoever was on the street."

"How so?" Jessica asked.

"I saw him coming between Beryl's and Hazel's houses not three minutes after the car drove off." Nadine hesitated, then said, "Well, maybe five or six minutes, but no longer."

"Okay, we'll talk to Henry, but later," Beryl said with a note of impatience. She motioned toward the living room. "Come on. Let's sit. I want to hear what went on with Jessica at the station this morning." Leading the way, she sat on one end of the sofa, patting the cushion beside her to indicate that Jessica should share the couch. Still feeling the effects of her own atypically active night and daytime nap, Beryl studied the young woman's face. "You were out late," she commented, "and up early this morning. Did you get any sleep at all?"

Carrying her coffee cup over to sit next to Beryl, Jessica shrugged. "A few hours. Woke early this morning and felt like a good long run. I sometimes use the track at the high school," she said, referring to the school yard a few blocks from the Sunnydale community. "The hour or so before dawn, the kids aren't using it."

"Did you see the smoke?" Nadine asked, handing Beryl a steaming mug of coffee before sitting in a small, overstuffed chair across the coffee table from her two guests. "Is that why you were at Sunnydale?"

"Actually, I heard the call on my scanner," Jessica explained. "I don't usually carry it, but I had a feeling that something was going to happen soon." She glanced at Beryl. "I mentioned it to you. That's why I was watching your neighbor's house last night."

"Well, your instincts were correct," Nadine declared before Beryl had a chance to reply. "Too bad all it did was get you into trouble."

"What did the police want with you?" Beryl asked, reminding them that the "trouble" was what she wanted to hear.

Jessica took a sip of coffee and turned to press her back into the corner of the couch, settling herself more comfortably. She was half turned toward Beryl, studying her over the rim of the mug. A few seconds lapsed before she lowered the cup. "You've obviously realized that they considered me a 'person of interest'," she said. There was no amusement in the statement, rather the young woman looked both sad and angry.

"You mean the police thought you set that fire?" Nadine demanded, upset that anyone could think ill of one of her brightest pupils.

Jessica nodded, turning her attention to Nadine. "Firefighters make good arsonists." This time there was a hint of irony in her tone. Her face softened as she explained, "It's actually not uncommon for a firefighter to start serious fires." Probably interpreting the amazement on Nadine's face, she hurried on. "Some are accidents. We who fight fires think we have everything under control, but fires can get out of hand very quickly."

"Not all who start the fires are that innocent," Beryl spoke up, drawing Jessica's eyes back to her.

"No," the young woman agreed. "Sorry to say, some firefighters have an urge to play the hero. They'll start a fire, then be the first or one of the first on the scene to contain it. Ta-daa. Instant hero," she said, her tone betraying her disapproval.

"So, how did you convince the police that you had nothing to do with setting this fire?" Beryl was curious.

"My captain showed up," Jessica said, trying unsuccessfully to hide a look of pleasure by taking another sip of coffee. "He's always been a decent boss, but I never expected him to come in and stick up for me like he did."

"The station chief?" Beryl said, her eyes widening in amazement and admiration. "Showed up in person?"

"Yup," Jessica said, this time unable to prevent the wide smile from lighting up her face. "Stormed right into the interview room and told 'em they were way off base." She sobered. "Then he and the lead detective left the room. A half hour later, the police let me go. Captain told me to go home and get some rest, but said I'd better be at my station on time for tomorrow's shift."

"Good man," Nadine muttered under her breath as Beryl asked her next question.

"Do you have your own suspect in mind?"

Jessica frowned and leaned forward to place her mug on the coffee table. "I can't say for certain, but I have my eye on some of the early responders I've seen at the other fires. I'd like to ask you about a couple of people, but please understand I have no evidence against anyone at this point, so I'd appreciate it if you keep this conversation confidential."

"Who have you seen?" Nadine wiggled to the edge of her chair, eager to hear who Jessica had in mind. Nadine herself had noticed several residents on the lawn when she'd arrived at the scene that morning, but had no idea which ones had been there first, except for Joey and Henry.

"Hold on," Jessica said, straightening up. "I don't want you to jump to conclusions just because I ask about someone you might know."

"Right," Beryl said, throwing Nadine a cautionary look before turning to Jessica. "Who'd you want to know about?"

Nadine shivered at the sentence construction, but refrained from commenting. She was too anxious to hear the answer to pull her schoolmarm routine.

"Henry Slater, for one," Jessica said, glancing from Beryl to Nadine.

"Henry?" Beryl asked, clearly astonished. Her surprise turned to thoughtfulness as she said to Nadine, "And you said he was at Hazel's house within minutes of you spotting the smoke."

Nadine nodded. "He's an old flirt, but I have trouble seeing him as an arsonist." When the other two turned to stare at her, Nadine felt her cheeks grow warm. "I'm not trying to defend him." In a quieter voice, she added, "I could be wrong."

"Is he capable of doing such a thing?" Jessica prompted.

Nadine thought for several seconds about the man she barely knew before she shook her head. "I guess I really can't say. I have no idea if he'd try to burn down someone's house."

Jessica swiveled her gaze to Beryl. "What do you think?"

Beryl shook her head. "Don't really know the man." Probably realizing Jessica wanted more, Beryl explained. "He's lived in the Big House for about two years now, maybe a little longer, but I don't spend a lot of time up here. I know folks to say hello to, but I don't know much about them." She wrinkled her nose as if smelling something bad. "Don't much care for gossips. They cause more trouble than not."

"I can ask around," Nadine offered. She raised an eyebrow at Beryl. "I don't mind chatting with an old gossip or two." More seriously, she added, "As with any rumor, we'll need to hear it from more than one person, particularly if they might be holding a grudge. I wouldn't want to flame the fire of someone's resentments."

"While you're poking around, find out if Henry and the Bennets were close, would you? I'd like to know if they knew each other before moving to Sunnydale." Beryl said.

Nadine remembered Mabel's accusation about Henry heading to Beryl's cottage. She nodded, certain she understood Beryl's motive for the request. If Nadine could verify a friendship between Henry and the Bennets, it would certainly put to rest any unseemly speculation connecting him with Beryl.

When no further discussion seemed to be forthcoming about Henry, Jessica turned to Beryl. "Do you know anything about Joe Marconi? Mrs. Rodd … er," she glanced across the coffee table. "*Nadine* said you were talking to him on your way here this afternoon."

"Joey?" Beryl looked thoughtful. "I know him better than Henry. Besides his duties as exercise instructor and personal trainer, Joey does odd jobs around Sunnydale, you know." When Jessica nodded that she had learned that much about the young man, Beryl went on. "He's done some work around my place. We've talked a bit." She narrowed her eyes. "You don't suspect *him*, do you?"

Jessica shrugged. "Not necessarily. As a matter of fact …" she paused, looking from Beryl to Nadine and back. "Can we keep this between ourselves? I don't want to spook whoever's setting these fires. If they go underground, we might never catch 'em." When the two women answered back simultaneously, "Of course" and "Absolutely," Jessica continued. "According to my captain, the investigators are pretty sure this morning's fire was not set by the same person who set the others in this area."

"What?" Beryl said.

"Wow," Nadine said.

Jessica nodded. "Arsonists have a definite fingerprint or MO, so we can usually tell when we're dealing with someone who's set more than one. Whoever started the fire in that bungalow not only didn't torch the other houses, but he or she didn't know much about what they were doing."

"Is that why there wasn't much damage?" Beryl asked.

"How do you know that?" Jessica asked, her expression showing her surprise.

Beryl shrugged. "Joey told me. That's one of the things I was talking to him about on my way here. He said most of the damage was caused by the smoke and water." She slid her gaze toward Nadine as if to say, *I told you what we talked about was important.*

"And who told him?" Jessica's stare was intense, questioning.

Beryl shrugged again. "Didn't ask. He had permission to be in the house, so I assume he spoke to someone in your department."

Nadine interrupted before they got off track. "Why wasn't there much damage?" she asked Jessica.

The young woman looked as if she wanted to question Beryl further, but after a second or two, she turned to explain to Nadine. "Whoever set the fire piled a bunch of papers in the middle of the bed and then dropped a lighted candle on them. Probably figured the whole place would go up in flames, there was so much smoke. The fire-retardant materials, particularly the bedspread, as well as the early call-in to the fire department, minimized the damage. As Beryl just said, most of the destruction was caused by water and smoke."

Nadine grew quiet, thinking about what Jessica had just revealed. Beryl hadn't much to say either. After a minute or two, Jessica broke the growing silence. "I know I'm sort of putting you on the spot, but I hope you'll help me get information about some of the residents. As I said before, I've seen a couple of them at the other fires, so I'm just following up. I hope I'm wrong, but it might be possible that we have a copy-cat. Maybe the empty house and my talk about an arsonist in the area was simply too much of a temptation."

Nadine gasped. "You don't really think one of the people living here ..." She felt so unnerved, she didn't know how to continue.

Beryl stepped into the silence. "I suppose that makes sense, since not a whole lot of people would have known it was empty, except for the Sunnydale residents, that is."

"Exactly," Jessica said. She looked relieved that her idea had been accepted. "If that's what we're dealing with, I'd like to stop him before he sets more fires."

"You asked about Joey," Beryl said, picking up the earlier conversation. "I know he was raised by his grandparents, his father's folks, after his own parents died in a car accident when he was twelve. He told me it was one of the reasons he came to work at Sunnydale. He likes older people, feels comfortable around them."

"That's nice," Nadine murmured. The others appeared not to have heard her.

"He wants to join the police force, become a detective eventually," Beryl continued. "He's been working hard to prepare for the exam … another reason he applied for the job here. He has unlimited use of the exercise equipment." She frowned at Jessica. "If you're looking at him for this fire in Hazel's bedroom, I would bet a year's pension he didn't do it."

In the silence that followed this declaration, the bell-like chiming of Nadine's mantelpiece clock filled the room. Beryl started. "Is it four o'clock already?" she declared and stood abruptly. "I've got to phone Doe Bennet, but first, I want to see if Stan is still in his office." Without further ado, she stood and hurried out of the apartment.

Chapter 15

Waiting impatiently for the elevator, Beryl thought about all she'd learned since waking up that afternoon. With macabre humor, she thought, *I shouldn't have gotten out of bed.* At that moment, she heard the echo of a door closing somewhere down a different hallway and the sound of voices approaching. *Of course, cocktail hour for some, early supper time for others,* she remembered. *That's why the elevator is taking an eternity to get here. Everyone's heading for the dining room.* She felt a stab of irritation. *I wouldn't be surprised if a Good Samaritan or two wasn't holding the elevator for stragglers.* With those thoughts and the desire to avoid having to make pleasant conversation with whomever was approaching the elevator, Beryl spun on her heel and hurried to the exit stairwell.

As she reached the next floor landing and began her descent to the lobby, she suddenly muttered "Shoot," as she recalled the administrative offices were on the second floor. Turning, she climbed back up to the landing. When her feet felt as if clad in lead instead of leather, she realized how unused to stairs she'd become, living in a single-story dwelling for the past dozen years. Rather than bursting through the door to the southern wing of the Big House, Beryl stumbled and held onto the metal railing for a moment to catch her breath. Precious moments, she thought as her heartbeat slowed. She hoped to catch Pemberly before he left the building. Otherwise, she'd have to wait until Monday to talk to him and that would delay her plans another day and a half.

With faltering steps, she reached the door to the managerial offices and cheered up instantly when she spotted Louise, Stan's secretary … or whatever title was politically correct these days. *I'll have to ask Louise one of these days*, she thought, *just not today*.

"Stan in?" huffed Beryl, hanging onto the doorknob.

The manager's personal assistant looked up and frowned with concern. "Are you all right, Beryl?" She started to rise from behind the desk, but Beryl waved her down.

"Gotta … speak … to Stan. He in?" she was beginning to catch her breath, but wasn't yet ready to speak in full sentences.

Louise picked up the receiver on her desk and pushed a few numbers while she spoke. "You missed him by ten minutes, but he may still be talking to our new receptionist." Abruptly her eyes unfocused as she dropped her gaze to the desktop. "Hi. Rachel?" After a second's pause, she said, "Is Stan still in the building?" Another second's pause. "Good. No, I don't need to speak with him, but tell him that Beryl Fishen does. Will you please ask him to wait? She'll be down shortly." Another couple of seconds went by before Louise said, "Thank you," replaced the receiver and turned to Beryl. "You're in luck."

Beryl nodded her gratitude and, having regained

her composure, thanked Louise and returned to the stairwell. She took her time and reached the lobby intact, ready to confer with Sunnydale's manager.

Nearing fifty, Stan was of medium height and overweight with thinning brown hair. He wouldn't turn heads, but he was competent and had worked on Sunnydale's administrative team since the community first opened, rising to his current position five years previously.

"Mrs. Fishen," he greeted Beryl formally. "Nice to see you." After exchanging pleasantries, he looked pointedly at his watch, then back to her face. His smile didn't reach his eyes. "What can I do for you?"

Noticing that Rachel, the new hire, was watching them and listening intently, Beryl gently took Stan's wrist and pulled him to a nearby cluster of overstuffed chairs, but didn't sit. Lowering her voice, she said, "I'll be calling Doe Bennet this evening. Before I do, I wanted to check with you and make sure you've told her about the fire."

"Yes, we have spoken, but unfortunately she won't be able to return here until mid-next week." Stan interrupted Beryl before she could finish her request. He didn't look happy about the news he'd just imparted as he went on to say, "When you speak with her, please remind her that the house needs to be cleared out so we can proceed with repairs as soon as possible. Thursday is the thirtieth, you know. If we run into next month, she'll have to pay the usual rent."

Beryl ignored the personal request, having heard what she'd not expected. Her heart leapt at the news that Doe wouldn't be returning for several days.

Beryl could take her time looking for any sign of what might have actually happened to her neighbor. What had gone on in that house over the past month … maybe more. And what about Joey's claim that the Bennets were imposters of some sort? They'd have time to search for proof of that accusation, as well.

"I think I can be of some assistance," Beryl said aloud, working to hide her delight at the unexpected reprieve. Her reply brought a brighter smile in return. Stan opened his mouth to speak, but she held up a hand. "I understand Kelsey is off somewhere at another audition, and I suspected it might not be convenient for Doe to get back here since she only just left for her own home. One reason I'll be phoning Doe is to offer to start packing up Hazel's belongings."

"Nice of you," Stan said with some enthusiasm. "As long you have Mrs. Bennet's approval … Anything we can do …" Apparently feeling the meaning of his unfinished sentences was clear … or perhaps he didn't want to actually commit himself … he seemed reassured and relieved. Glancing again at his watch when he spoke, he started to turn away.

She stopped him with a hand on his arm. "I'd like Joey's help," she said quickly. "Can you spare him for a few hours?" In a flash of brilliance that she knew would appeal to Stan and assure his cooperation, she added, "With his handyman's knowledge of the place, he'd be perfect for making a preliminary assessment of the damage."

Stan's eyes lit up with the thought, as Beryl had anticipated. "Fine. Sure. Okay with me," he said and attempted to free himself from her hold.

"I'd also like to set up a memorial service for George and Hazel," Beryl said, tightening her grasp on the material of his suitcoat sleeve. "That's the other thing I wanted to check. You haven't planned anything for them yet, have you?"

"I don't think so, but you'd better ask Louise." This time, Stan successfully pulled away, but only because Beryl was ready to loosen her grip.

"Thank you," she called to his back as he hastened toward the front doors and freedom.

Mentally rubbing her hands together that she could get on with her plans, she waved to Rachel and walked more slowly after the Sunnydale director. At this hour, she preferred not to walk through the dining room. In order to avoid being stopped by residents who would certainly ask about Hazel, Beryl skirted the building from the front portico, past the courtyard and walked the short distance across the lawn to her house. As she approached her patio, she looked over at the boarded-up window and smoke blackened siding of her neighbor's bungalow. Her thoughts returned to Hazel. Beryl was deeply troubled by the news Butch had relayed.

Chapter 16

Once her guests had gone, Nadine could hardly wait to begin her investigation. After listening to Beryl talk about her late husband's work on the police force, Nadine had found, little by little, she paid more attention to the goings-on around her. She'd also developed an unusual talent for observation she hadn't known she'd possessed. Temporarily warmed by the certainty that her own husband would have been proud of her, she turned her mind to the task ahead. Wondering how she could learn anything about Henry without encouraging his advances … a thought that made her shudder … she decided to have supper in the main floor dining room instead of cooking something in her own kitchen. She would first see how much she could glean by simply mingling with other Big House residents.

Downstairs, she was not surprised to see Mabel Gladstone sitting at her usual table next to the floor-to-ceiling windows where she had an uninterrupted view of both the backyard patio and the dining room. This evening, Nadine was relying on the old gossip's insatiable curiosity as she noted the woman squinting merrily at residents from her favored spot. Nadine was mentally planning her strategy to wheedle information from Mabel as she pretended to peruse the menu, waiting for the attendant to finish with the couple in front of her. Suddenly, she felt her cheeks begin to glow and realized, with some shock, she was experiencing a stab of conscience. At that moment, she felt slightly less critical of Mabel and considered herself a bit more hypocritical. Maybe she wasn't cut out to be a snoop.

The white-coated young woman asked for her order just then, giving Nadine no time to dwell on the question. She asked for the chicken special before hastening toward Mabel's table, giving herself no more time to examine the ethics of her situation. She reminded herself that she would take whatever the old chatterbox told her with a grain of salt. The possibly outrageous rumors about Henry or anyone else would merely be a place to start, and she expected to verify any information she uncovered with at least two other sources, as per the recommended scientific method she'd learned from a fellow high school teacher. She thought it especially wise in this situation, given Mabel's handicaps. Remembering the last piece of chatter from the woman, Nadine wondered if the man Mabel had seen crossing the lawn toward Beryl's house had really been Henry at all.

Typically, Mabel's myopic eyes held a gleam of anticipation. "Do join me, won't you?" she invited, extending a hand, palm up, toward the opposite seat. When polite preliminary exchanges had been made, the nosy woman leaned into the table as if to share a secret, but didn't lower her voice. "Was Beryl Fishen up to see you?" Before Nadine could answer, Mabel went on with barely a pause, "I saw her talking to

Stan Pemberly a little while ago. She almost never comes up here, so I figure it must be about that fire this morning. Isn't it a shame what happened to those poor Bennets. Such a tragedy that three in one family are gone in less than a year."

To Nadine's relief, their waiter approached and placed a plate in front of Mabel, obliging her to sit back in her chair and take a breath. When he removed the metal cover from the plate, Nadine saw that her dinner companion had ordered the same menu special that Nadine herself had requested—chicken parmesan with spaghetti and fresh green beans. She hadn't realized how hungry she was until the aroma of cheese and tomato sauce floated up. Happily, a second attendant placed her serving before her a moment later.

Silence descended as the two women took their first bites. Nadine was then about to sip from her water glass when she noticed Mabel bestowing her brightest smile to someone over Nadine's left shoulder. A second later, she hallooed and beckoned with an upraised hand wave. "Yoo hoo, Henry. Come join us."

Nadine's appetite diminished as the sharp scent of Henry's aftershave wafted toward her when he took the chair next to hers. "Please don't stand on ceremony," he said, eyeing the dinner plates. "It looks delicious. Don't let it get cold." As the ladies resumed eating, he added, "How is it? I almost ordered the parmesan myself, but decided on the tilapia. Better for my waist line, you know," he said, turning to smile at Nadine.

If her appetite had been about to return, Henry's

words took away any further pleasure. She wondered if he'd been waiting to show himself until she began to eat and hence had no chance to think up an excuse for rushing away. How in the world was she to question Mabel about Henry when he was sitting beside her? At Mabel's next words, Nadine realized another opportunity had presented itself and silently wished she had more of Beryl's investigative savvy.

"I was just saying what a tragedy that the Bennets all passed in such a short time."

"Yes," Henry managed before leaning back in his chair when a waiter appeared with his plate.

Grabbing her chance when the other two fell momentarily silent, Nadine asked, "How long did you know them before moving to Sunnydale?" She figured it was better to phrase her question with the presumption, along the lines of the old joke, "How often do you beat your wife?"

Henry stared at her with a curious expression for several seconds, then broke into a wide smile. "Is that what Beryl asked you to find out?" he said.

Nadine felt her cheeks flame. He had probably been fishing with his question, just as she had, but he hadn't blushed. She had never been good at hiding her feelings. Roger used to laugh at how transparent she could be. Now, however, in an attempt to cover her guilt, she widened her eyes. "What makes you think that?"

Henry chuckled and turned back to his food as he spoke. "Because she was here at the Big House this afternoon, probably came to see you. I doubt you have as much interest in her next door neighbors as she would. Did you ever meet George or Hazel?"

Nadine hated that he dismissed her so handily. All the more reason to reject his advances in the future. His flirting always made her uncomfortable, even though she knew he acted the same with all women. She suspected he held her in no more regard than of the other women with whom he flirted. *Odious man*, she thought, suddenly wondering, with little regret, if her nosiness might cool his attentions. She bent her head to concentrate on her own supper and became aware that Mabel had been quietly watching them both. *She's enjoying herself,* Nadine thought with rising irritation, angry with herself for blowing her cover as much as with Mabel for being witness to her discomfort.

"Come now," Henry said, a tone of joviality back in his voice. "I'm sure we can work something out to everyone's satisfaction. Have a drink with me later and I'll tell you whatever you wish to know," he teased.

Annoyed at his self-assurance and condescending attitude, Nadine reached for her water glass and took a sip. With a flash of returning humor, she thought for an instant of spitting a stream at him, but refrained from the childhood prank she had used on a few occasions in spats with her younger brother. She hadn't been able to slap the toddler, but she had soaked him a time or two. Instantly coming to her senses, she swallowed and felt her composure return with a determination not to allow Henry to unsettle her.

"You're wrong," she said, dabbing her mouth with a napkin as she stalled for time to consider. "I do care about Hazel. Yes, Beryl came to see me this afternoon, but not to ask me to interrogate you." *It's not always about you, Henry*, Nadine wanted to say. Instead, she confessed, "She wants me to help organize a memorial service for the Bennets. Since I didn't know the couple, I thought I'd interview those who might have been close to the Bennets. It will help me get to know them better, so I can create a more meaningful commemorative." Nadine hoped she sounded convincing as she prattled on. "I've heard that you were good friends with George Bennet and that you'd known each other for quite some time."

Henry tilted his head to study her with what seemed like renewed interest. Even though she had distracted him and seemed to regain a semblance of his trust, Nadine's stomach roiled. Beryl owes me for this, she thought, wondering if she would ever shake the man's persistent advances now.

"Hen-REE!" came a shrill voice across the dining room. "There you are."

Nadine looked across the table as Clara and her entourage came bustling up to stand beside him. Mabel was in her element, sitting back in her chair, beaming as her eyes darted around the players in this small drama.

"You naughty man," cooed Clara. "I thought you were going to join us on the patio for a drink before dinner." She looked down her nose at the single empty seat beside Mabel. "And you didn't even save a table for us."

Henry took his time putting down his fork and wiping his mouth on the napkin before gazing over at Clara. "Why don't you grab that table," he said, nodding toward the center of the room where a waiter was in the process of clearing away used dishes. "When I'm finished here, I'll join you for dessert." He spoke in a low, calm voice, offsetting her shrill tone.

Beneath Clara's makeup, Nadine noticed a slight reddening of the woman's cheeks and neck. Clearly, she was unaccustomed to being put off. "Come, ladies," she said to her companions as she spun on her heel and flounced away.

Henry picked up his fork and resumed eating. By now, Nadine had lost her appetite completely. Mabel, having cleaned her plate, leaned toward Nadine and said in her loud voice, "I knew Hazel. You can interview me." With a brisk nod of her head as if to say *I'm really the only person you need to ask,* she continued. "Knew her from the book club. After we read *Aquarius Revisited* … you know the one where the author interviewed a bunch of people who were considered rebels in the nineteen-sixties? Well, Hazel must have been feeling as nostalgic as me because we had quite a talk about the old days."

Nadine mentally heard fingernails running down a chalkboard at the pronoun and was about to blurt out "nostalgic as *I*" when Henry intervened. "Really? What memories did she talk about? Was she with the demonstrators in Chicago at the Democratic National Convention?"

Nadine looked at him and wondered if he were being facetious. The impression Nadine had from the little she knew of Hazel Bennet, *radical* was not a word she would have used to describe the woman. Nadine was even more curious as to why Henry would mention Chicago. Was that where the Bennets had lived? Had Henry really known them before moving to Sunnydale? It had been a guess on her part, mainly to goad him.

She was about to ask him again how long he and the Bennets had been friends, but the opportunity was destroyed by a waiter who approached the table to ask Mabel if he could take her plate away. The server then looked at Nadine's hardly touched meal. "Was something wrong with your food, Mrs. Rodd?" The young man seemed genuinely concerned.

"No, no," Nadine said, handing him her dish. "I didn't seem to be as hungry as I thought." The moment had clearly been killed.

Henry leaned back to allow the waiter to take his own empty plate before tilting his head toward Clara and her friends. "Bring my coffee and pudding to Mrs. Fairchild's table, would you, Kevin?" Once the young man had acquiesced and headed back to the kitchen, Henry turned to Mabel. "I'm interested in what Hazel had to say about the old days. Shall we meet later on the patio? It's a great night to sit out, but you may need a sweater. I'll go visit my friends over there and meet you outside in an hour." He faced Nadine and leaned slightly toward her, preparatory to rising. "How about you. Will you join us in reminiscing about the good ole days?"

Nadine thought it a splendid idea. She also wanted to learn what Mabel had to say … *and* she was determined to find out how well Henry had known the Bennets. So far, he had avoided her question.

Chapter 17

While Nadine was sitting with her companions in the dining room of the Big House, Beryl was on the phone to Doe Bennet. "I thought you'd like to know that I found Smudge," she said after identifying herself ... in case Doe hadn't examined Caller ID before picking up. Beryl was then going to reveal where she'd found the cat, hoping to stir a bit of guilt in the woman for shutting the poor creature in the crawl space, but Doe didn't give her the chance.

"That's nice," the woman returned, sounding distracted. "I can't be bothered with a cat, so if you'll take him to an animal shelter, I'll settle up any charges you incur after George and Hazel's estate is settled." Caught off guard at the cold dismissal of Hazel's beloved pet, Beryl was speechless long enough for Doe to ask, "Was that all?" Perhaps she then felt a pang of conscience for she added quickly, "Look, Beryl, I appreciate your phoning, but I'm in the middle of a crisis here. The tenants vacated one of my rentals without notifying me. They also neglected to tell me about a water leak that has caused extensive damage not only to my rental, but also to the condo below."

Beryl barely listened to Doe's troubles. She was stunned that the woman would abandon the cat with so little feeling. Even if Doe didn't realize black cats are extremely difficult to adopt out, she might consider that condemning Smudge to a shelter could mean the end of him. Granted, Smudge wasn't Doe's pet, but certainly she'd have developed *some* compassion for the cat after being around him for the past month. If not, at least loyalty to Hazel who had adored the feline would dictate some sort of effort to find him a good home. Doe hadn't even bothered to ask Beryl if she'd want to keep Smudge or if she knew of someone who would.

Her anger beginning to boil over the woman's heartlessness, nevertheless, Beryl was aware when Doe stopped to take a breath. Quickly, Beryl cut in, trying to hide her contempt, but displaying a hint of sarcasm. "Sorry to hear about your problems. You must be at your wit's end, what with the fire down here as well."

"I don't even want to think about *that* disaster right now," Doe whined. She sounded as if she were becoming increasingly agitated. "It's impossible for me to leave here for another few days. I understand the house has been boarded up until I can deal with it. Honestly, Beryl, I don't need any more complications right now."

"That's another reason I'm phoning," Beryl jumped in, relieved that her plan was falling into place so easily. She would stick with what mattered to Doe and not mention her wish to adopt Smudge. That question already seemed to have been answered. "If you'll permit me, I'll go over to the house and start cleaning things up. You know, get rid of damaged goods and organize Hazel's belongings so you'll only have to look them over and decide what you want to do with them." She continued when Doe didn't speak at once. "Assuming you don't want any of her clothing or bedding or household things, I can arrange for charities to take them and give you tax receipts. Of course, personal things like jewelry, bank records and personal papers, I'd put aside for you."

Apparently, that got Doe's attention. She must not have been expecting such a generous offer because she stammered slightly. "Well ... um ... that's very good of you." After a brief pause, during which time Beryl held her breath and waited, Doe finally said, "That's really a wonderful offer. Very kind of you. I can certainly use the help. I'd ask Kelsey to assist, but you know how busy she is, flying back and forth to auditions. Besides, she's no good at that sort of thing. I'm sure she'd only get in your way."

No good at what? Auditioning or cleaning? Beryl was tempted to ask, but refrained from making any sarcastic remark about the young woman to her mother. Kelsey wasn't good for much that didn't require a mirror, Beryl imagined.

"I don't think she expected to be back in Denver until tomorrow, anyway." Doe's words interrupted Beryl's irreverent musings.

From her brief encounters with Doe's daughter, Beryl had pegged Kelsey as a spoiled only-child whose mother indulged her. At least when the Bennets were alive, they held back the funds necessary to finance the young woman's vain attempts to land an acting job. The only reason she hadn't moved either to New York City or Los

Angeles was because Doe hadn't yet agreed to pay the rent for an apartment, not until Kelsey had some means to buy her own clothes and groceries, at the very least. Beryl remembered Hazel's theory that the reason wasn't so much that Doe wanted Kelsey to be responsible as that Doe couldn't bear to cut the apron strings. Beryl was again brought back to the conversation by Doe's voice.

"Thank you for your offer, Beryl. I accept with gratitude. You've taken a huge weight off my shoulders. I'm sure you can get a key from that manager. What's his name?" Without waiting for an answer, Doe continued. "If you'll excuse me, now, I have another call coming in."

"Of course," Beryl said and wondered if Doe had heard her or if she'd already switched off. Either way, Beryl didn't mind in the least. She'd gotten the permission she wanted. Smiling at her own cleverness, she returned the cordless to its cradle.

The next few hours dragged. Waiting impatiently for Joey to get off work, she tried to keep busy. She fed the cat and herself and puttered around the house doing odd jobs like dusting the lamps and wiping down the bathroom sink. At one point, she thought of going over to start looking around before Joey arrived, but when she thought of the footsteps she'd heard overhead when she'd been in the crawl space, she immediately rejected the idea. The last thing she wanted was to come face to face with an ill-intentioned stranger when she was alone in the empty house. Trying to rid her mind of the previous night's memory, she settled for mentally roaming the Bennets' bungalow, planning on how she'd conduct her search.

This time, she intended to go carefully through all the closets to make certain she hadn't missed spotting her coat the last time she'd been in the house. She also wanted to go through the bathrooms and kitchen to see if she could find any suspicious substance that might have caused Hazel's rapid deterioration. The extent of her dehydration had been shocking.

Beryl considered what she knew, or at least, what she'd been told by Doe about Hazel's condition. According to the daughter-in-law, Hazel suffered severe eye pain, a condition that began shortly before George's death. That was why the poor woman had to lie in a darkened room and would often refuse to see visitors or accept phone calls. Beryl winced at the thought of such agony.

She then mulled over what Butch had told her about the coroner's analysis after the preliminary examination of the body. When contacted, Hazel's personal physician had been puzzled by the report of an unusual amount of hydrochlorothiazide in the woman's system. He had never prescribed the medication for either of the elderly Bennets, but had remembered a year or so previously, writing a prescription for their son. On that occasion, when Steven was visiting his parents, he'd run out of his blood pressure medication. After conferring with the younger Bennet's cardiologist, the local medical man had refilled the prescription.

Beryl was trying to figure out if or why Hazel would be taking her son's medication when she heard tapping on the glass slider. Tucking the problem to the back of her mind, she hurried to greet Joey and accompany him to Hazel's house. As she stepped out onto the flagstones, a brisk wind caught her unaware and caused her to consider going back inside to fetch a coat. The thought brought to mind the coat that was hanging in her garage.

"Wait a minute, Joey," she said and reentered the house. On her way through the kitchen and out to the garage, she grew more satisfied with her plan. She was certain the coat belonged to one of the women next door, so why not get it out of her garage and hang it in the closet at Hazel's. Taking it off the hanger, Beryl shoved a hand into one side pocket and then the other, wanting to make certain nothing had been overlooked during her previous inspection. In the second pocket, much to her surprise, her fingers touched something hard and rough, tucked into the back corner.

She held the object toward the light of the garage's only fixture. Even in that dimly lighted room, she knew the earring was something expensive. Hurrying back to the kitchen, she studied the jewel more closely under brighter light. What she had in her hand was a cluster drop earring of sapphires with tiny diamond accents. Setting it carefully on the counter, Beryl stared at the precious stones while she again went through the coat pockets. She then ran the hem and cuffs through her fingers to see if she could find the matching earring or anything else that might have gotten caught in the fabric or fallen through a tear. There was nothing else to be found.

"What's taking you so long?" Joey asked, walking toward her from the living room.

Beryl looked up quickly and, in an instant, decided to keep the discovery to herself until she could think what to do. Did it belong to Doe or Kelsey? Perhaps it had belonged to a previous owner and overlooked for years. Obviously, it was far more valuable than the coat in which it had been found. She raised the garment. Not wanting to go into a long story of how she'd come by the coat, she simply explained, "This belongs to Doe. I thought I'd better hang it in Hazel's front hall closet so I don't forget to give it back to her."

Joey gave a compliant shrug. "Okay. Let's go then," he said, leading the way out to the patio and over to the neighboring house. Once inside, he switched on the living room lights after receiving assurance from Beryl for the third time that they had both Doe Bennet's permission and Stan Pemberly's blessing to be there. "No sense groping around in the dark," he said with a nervous laugh.

"Whew," Beryl complained as she breathed in the foul air. "Maybe if we shut the bedroom door, we can block out some of that smoky odor."

"Too bad I boarded up the window. Do you think I should remove the plywood tomorrow, so that room can air out?" he asked Beryl.

"It might not be a bad idea, but maybe you can rig it so we can take it off during the day and put it back at night. I wouldn't want anyone getting in and doing more damage than what's been done already. Until we go through things, I don't even know what valuables are still here." Beryl was thinking aloud more than speaking to Joey. "For now, let's just do a preliminary once-over. If we find something that seems to have promise, we'll put it aside to examine later." She was thinking of evidence in a medical death, but knew he was thinking of a possible identity cover-up.

"Where should we start?" Joey asked returning to the living room after going to close off the fire-damaged bedroom.

"Why don't you start with this room and then check the kitchen. I might as well begin searching closets after I hang up this coat," Beryl said. "If you're looking for papers, go through all the drawers you can find. Look in any boxes you come across. I'll check the ones in the closets. People tend to store personal papers and pictures in shoe boxes."

The plan was a good one and in less than an hour, the pair had covered nearly all of the rooms. After quickly poking her head into Hazel's burned bedroom, Beryl decided to leave the wet and smoky remnants for the next day and went on to the second bedroom.

"Guest room," Joey observed, eyeing the twin beds. "This must have been where Doe and Kelsey slept. Do you think it's worth searching in here?"

"Why not?" Beryl asked, only half listening to him.

"Can't imagine George hiding anything in a spare room where anyone staying here might find it."

"Let's give it a toss, anyway," Beryl encouraged. "Doe and Kelsey haven't completely moved out yet, so be careful and leave everything the way you found it."

Joey hesitated, looking around the room at the lone three-drawer bureau against one wall and the bedside table that stood between the two headboards. "I'll take that one," he said nodding at the narrow table with one drawer. A low shelf held several books and a smattering of papers. "You can go through their clothes." Sitting on the farther bed with his back to the door, he opened the shallow drawer.

Still determined to find her coat, Beryl ignored the bureau and moved to the closet, sliding aside the right-hand panel. There were no garments on hangers, but a medium-sized suitcase stood on the floor. Gripping the handle, she dragged the bag out into the room. It was too heavy for her to lift, so she left it on the carpet. Joey glanced across the other bed as she bent to flick the latches on either side of the handle.

"What'd you find?" he asked, looking up from the small notebook he'd picked up.

"Probably nothing," Beryl replied distractedly as she realized it would be far easier to go through the contents if the case was on the bed instead of the floor. Grasping the handle with one hand and the lip of the lid with the other, she attempted to swing it up. Her uneasy handhold slipped as the suitcase caught the edge of the mattress. The impact caused her to drop the box and spill its contents.

"What are you doing?" The shrill, angry voice came from the doorway as Kelsey Martine burst into the room.

Beryl glanced up, startled by the young woman's sudden appearance. Ordinarily, she probably would have felt some guilt over being caught snooping where she didn't belong, but she'd returned her gaze to the mass of objects at her feet. On top of the assortment of dresses, shoes and toiletries lay a full-length black coat with silver buttons. Briefly looking over to frown at Kelsey who glared back, Beryl bent and picked up the garment. She held it up, turning the coat so Kelsey could see the front.

"This is my coat," Beryl accused. "You stole my coat."

"Those are my audition clothes and look what you've done," Kelsey blustered, stomping around the beds to Beryl's side with hands curled into tight fists.

Joey, who had frozen in place, rose as if he would need to subdue the woman, but Beryl showed him a palm, signaling him to stay where he was.

"You took my new coat and left me your old tattered one," she said, keeping her voice low and even this time. She was disciplining a recalcitrant child, even though the young woman was at least 18, if not 19 years old.

"I was going to give it back," Kelsey insisted, as if she had every right to take whatever she wanted.

"What were you doing at the theater?" Beryl asked. Not that it mattered, but she was curious.

"Mother told me to go see when they'll be bringing in a new play." Kelsey pouted. "She says there's no more money for plane tickets, so I have to audition within driving distance."

Beryl kept her temper in check when she said, "So you thought you'd do some coat shopping while you were there, did you?"

Kelsey frowned and stamped her foot. "Of course not. It's not my fault that you hung your black coat next to mine. I told the girl which one to get and she gave me that." Kelsey loosened a fist enough to point a well-manicured finger at the garment Beryl had draped over her arm. "I was going to tell her it wasn't mine, but it fit me, so I figured I'd borrow it." She narrowed her eyes at Beryl and said, "You have your coat back, so what's the big deal. Now I want mine. Where is it?"

Beryl tipped her chin toward the open bedroom door. "It's in the closet by the front door." Then, unable to hide her curiosity over the incongruity of Kelsey wearing such a decrepit rag, Beryl asked, "Where did you get your coat?" leaving out any hint as to her distaste for the item in question.

The young woman frowned, and Beryl thought for a minute that Kelsey wasn't going to answer. Finally, giving a one-shoulder shrug, she said, "In Calgary where I was auditioning a couple of weeks ago. It's cold in Canada. I needed a coat." She shrugged again and crouched to grab a dress from the floor and drop it into the suitcase.

Ahhh, Beryl thought as light dawned. S*he took it from the wardrobe collection. That would explain the smell and the stains around the collar. Many actors must have sweated in that coat beneath hot stage lights that would also have melted their makeup.* Unable to resist the temptation to needle the spoiled child, she said, "You planning to return it?"

Kelsey didn't answer. Instead, she continued to stuff items back into her luggage. "What are you doing in this house, anyway?" she said without looking up. Some of her earlier anger returned, but her tone had lost impact, and she sounded more petulant than accusatory.

Disregarding the fact that she and Joey probably

had no business including the spare room in their mission, Beryl said, "Your mother knows we're here. I'm organizing the house's contents for her." A sudden thought struck her. "Are you staying here tonight?" she asked, tossing Joey a worried look. They still had the garage to search, if they were to be thorough.

"Are you kidding?" Kelsey's high-pitched question revealed her disgust. "All that smoke from the fire. This place smells like a dirty ashtray. I'm staying at a hotel."

Relieved that Kelsey seemed to have no further interest in their presence, Beryl wondered if the young woman felt any guilt at all over having been caught with stolen property. She guessed the brat had never held a single unselfish thought in her life.

Kelsey had finished her task except to scoop up cosmetic paraphernalia that had scattered from a small, unzipped travel bag. She scowled up at Beryl and snapped, "I'm driving to Grand Junction tomorrow and I'm going to tell Mother I found you going through our things."

"You do that," Beryl replied, unable to prevent a smile and a shrug at Joey when Kelsey's attention refocused on closing the suitcase. The young man's eyes were wide. He appeared to be holding his breath.

With a final grunt and a snap of the last catch, Kelsey rose and, with the handle clutched in both hands, she spun. Head high, she shuffled out of the room with what little dignity she could muster.

"Whew," Beryl sighed when she heard first the closet and then the front door slam a few minutes later. She tossed her newly recovered coat onto the bed and dropped down next to it. For a split second, the image of flowers flashed through her head, so quickly she almost missed it. Blinking her eyes and giving a small shake of her head at the incongruity of the moment, she half turned to face Joey and sputtered a short laugh. "Had enough for tonight?" she asked. "Let's save the garage for tomorrow." Suddenly, she wanted to get out of the Bennets' house.

Joey took a deep breath and let it out slowly, then chuckled. "You sure make a better actress than she does. Do you really think she'll tell her mother we were going through her things?"

Beryl shook her head. "Whether she does or not, we have Doe's permission to be here. If Doe complains, we'll deal with the issue later."

Indicating the bedside table, Joey changed the subject. "I'm okay with leaving anything else for tomorrow, but I'm almost done with this drawer." He nodded at the dresser. "Don't you want to look through the bureau before we go?"

Beryl felt weary after the confrontation with Kelsey, but she agreed. "Guess we'd better not leave any stone unturned." She put her hands on her knees and leaned slightly, prepared to stand when her eyes caught a small greenish-blue object on the floor. "What's this?" she remarked aloud, bending to retrieve a capsule from the carpet. "It must have fallen from Kelsey's bag." Placing her feet carefully, she stood and turned in a slow circle, studying the floor and finding two more pills. "Ever seen these before?" she asked Joey, moving between the beds to place one in his palm.

He examined it, turning it over in his fingers. "Can't say as I have. Maybe she's on some sort of tranquilizer," he added, handing the capsule back.

Beryl slipped her finds into the pocket of her slacks. "I'll show them to Butch. Maybe he can tell me. Or I might ask at one of the local drugstores," she said as she returned to the task of investigating the bureau drawers.

Finished with their hasty examination, the two were about to leave the house when Beryl remembered the shelves. With her newly retrieved coat folded over one forearm, she took hold of Joey's wrist and pulled him toward the laundry room. She waved a hand to indicate the built-in structure next to the stacked washer and dryer. "Did you do this for George and Hazel?"

Joey shook his head. "Not me. I bet George put these up. He did most of the inside work himself. Called on me only when he needed an extra pair of hands."

"Can you build something like that for me?" she asked. "I especially like this step at the bottom. They used it to raise Smudge's food and water off the floor, and I'd like to do the same." She indicated the long box serving as the lowest shelf, approximately the size and shape of a stair tread.

"Sure, I can do this," Joey said. He bent to smooth a hand over the surface that had been covered with a strip of grayish-brown carpeting. Running his fingers along the lip of the shelf, he suddenly frowned and dropped to his knees. He studied the underside of the inch-long overhang before looking up with a grin while he fiddled with whatever he'd discovered. "Did you want storage space underneath, like this," he said, lifting the top. The board rose smoothly and soundlessly to reveal a small, steel safe. George had installed the foot-wide box on its back so the digital panel was facing up for easy access.

"Wow. What a great hiding place," Beryl said, examining the back of the lid where hidden hinges had been deftly placed and the front where hooks and eyes had been set so as to be invisible to anyone standing. "What do you suppose he kept in the safe?" she wondered aloud.

Joey's eyes were twinkling. "I bet the evidence Henry was talking about is in here." He looked at her with a less hopeful expression. "Don't suppose you know the combination."

She couldn't help but laugh at his downcast look, although she felt his frustration. "Hardly. I didn't even know this was anything other than a simple shelf for feeding the cat." She moved the coat aside so she could see her watch. "It's after nine and I'm too exhausted to think. Let's come back tomorrow. I found my coat, but now I'm committed to packing up this house, so we can work on breaking into this thing another time."

Beryl went to the sliding doors while Joey turned off all the lights except for the outside patio fixture. She waited on the flagstones while he locked up. Turning with him toward her own cottage, she was startled by a figure stepping from the shadows of the large blue spruce at the corner of the yard.

"What have you two been up to in the Bennets' house?" Henry Slater asked.

Chapter 18

"Where's Smudge?" Nadine asked, glancing down at the partially empty food bowl. She'd been looking forward to greeting the cat after Beryl had invited her to breakfast and a confab Sunday morning. Nadine had been thinking of fostering a cat from one of the local shelters, a resolve that had strengthened since Beryl assumed custody of Hazel's orphaned black feline.

"Taking over my bed," Beryl replied from where she was standing at the stove. "Poor thing must have been used to sleeping with Hazel. I didn't put him in the laundry room last night, but I did shut him out of my bedroom. In the middle of the night, he kept scratching at the door, so I opened it just to get some peace." She turned her attention back to the bacon she was cooking and spoke over her shoulder. "He came out for breakfast earlier, but now he's probably stretched out on my extra pillow which he seems to have claimed for his own." She laughed. "I'd forgotten just how much room a cat can take up. When I woke this morning, I was practically clinging to the edge of my queen-size mattress and Smudge was lying full-length with all four paws in the middle of my back." Removing the bacon to a plate, she swapped one frying pan for a smaller one in which butter was already melting. "By the way," she changed the subject abruptly as she reached for the bowl of beaten eggs and turned her head briefly to toss a mischievous look at Nadine. "Ran into your friend Henry last night."

Nadine refused to show the surprise she knew Beryl expected. Feeling almost no curiosity, she replied, "Oh? And where was that?"

"Lurking outside Hazel's house. He literally slithered out of the shadows, like some character out of an old B-rated movie. Startled the heck out of Joey and me when we were standing on Hazel's patio." Beryl lost her smile.

"Joey was at Hazel's again last night?" Nadine asked, raising her eyebrows. "I assumed from what you said yesterday afternoon, he'd finished going through the house?" She paused a moment as something else occurred to her. "What were *you* doing there?"

Still holding the bowl and keeping an eye on the heating pan, Beryl gave Nadine the short version. "When I called Doe to tell her about Smudge, she complained about some business problems in Grand Junction and said she wouldn't be able to get back here for a few more days." Beryl gave an off-handed shrug as she continued, "I offered to help pack up the house and asked Joey to come with me. We were leaving and locking up when Henry surprised us." Saying no more, she focused her attention on the stove as she poured the egg batter into the hot pan.

"Was this one of Henry's night-time excursions that Mabel witnessed a while back?" Nadine asked. So far, she hadn't been able to uncover a single piece of gossip about the man. He seemed very secretive. She wondered if he might be dangerous.

Beryl remained quiet while she finished cooking the eggs, dividing them between two plates to which she added slices of bacon and toast. She brought the food to the counter and placed a dish in front of Nadine. "He said he'd come out of the Big House to enjoy the night air and saw lights on in the Bennets' cottage. *Obviously*," she added with heavy sarcasm as she sat down to her own breakfast, "he felt it his duty to check on the house." She picked up a wedge of toast, bit into it and chewed thoughtfully before she swallowed and asked. "Did you find out anything new after I left yesterday?"

"Not much, but I brought you something that may be useful to our investigation." Nadine jumped up from her chair and scurried around the counter to the living room where she'd left a tote bag on the overstuffed chair. Reaching inside, she pulled out the object she'd wrapped in a large handkerchief. "Ta-daa," she crowed, holding it up as she returned to her seat. Placing it carefully between their two breakfast plates, she said, "Don't touch."

Biting off a piece of bacon, Beryl eyed the thing, then slid her eyes to Nadine. "What is it?"

"Fingerprints," Nadine announced and felt as smug as the Cheshire Cat. "Henry Slater's fingerprints."

"Pretty big for finger prints, wouldn't you say," Beryl teased.

"Oh, Beryl," Nadine said with a laugh and a swat on her friend's upper arm. "It's one of Sunnydale's tumblers. His fingerprints are on the glass." She felt her stomach lurch with sudden uncertainty. "At least, I think they are. I hope I didn't wipe them off when I wrapped it in Ralph's old hankie."

"How did you manage to get a glass with Henry's prints on it?" Beryl asked, not wanting to discourage her friend … at least not until it could be determined whether or not she'd successfully gotten a good set of prints.

"I did it last night," Nadine said, feeling her enthusiasm return. "Good ole Clara came through again, unwittingly as usual." Nadine proceeded to tell Beryl about having dinner with Mabel when Henry showed up. "I didn't know what to expect when he asked me to join them in the courtyard afterwards, but I didn't want to miss what Mabel had to say about her conversation with Hazel."

"What did she say?" Beryl asked, her eyes flashing with anticipation.

"I'll get to that." Nadine scowled, not liking the interruption when she was trying to explain how clever she'd been. "First, I want to tell you how I got the glass."

"Sorry," Beryl apologized. "Go ahead. I'll try to keep still, but cut to the chase, will you?"

Feeling as if some of the wind had gone out of her sails, Nadine went on. "Mabel and I got to the courtyard only a few minutes before Henry came out with a tray of after-dinner drinks. Snifters of brandy, all around. He probably thought that Mabel's tongue would be even looser with liquor," Nadine said with a laugh, "and it was." When Beryl produced only a silent smile, Nadine continued. "Actually, Mabel didn't have that much to tell, if you want the truth. I think she made a big to-do over nothing, just to get attention. You know how she is."

Nadine noticed Beryl's lips tighten and hurried back to the subject. "What Mabel told us was basically what you already know. The Bennets moved here from Seattle about three years ago. After their son had his first heart attack, Hazel insisted they live closer to their only child, so they moved to Colorado."

Beryl raised her hand in a silent request to speak.

Nadine chuckled at the gesture that brought back schoolroom memories. "Yes, Miss Fishen?" Nadine spoke as she would have to one of her students.

Beryl ignored the act. "As you said, I already know most of what you've told me about George and Hazel. They didn't follow their son to the western slope at that time because George's diabetes had just been diagnosed and his condition had to be stabilized. Tragically, Steven suffered his fatal heart attack before George and Hazel could decide whether or not they wanted to move again." Beryl paused briefly before switching her attention back to Sunnydale's news source. "Didn't Mabel have anything earth-shattering to tell you?"

"Since I don't know what else you might know about the Bennets ..." Nadine huffed, leaving the sentence unfinished. She was disappointed that Beryl wasn't showing more gratitude for the information. Then, feeling childish for sulking, she decided just to get on with her story and ignore her friend's lack of appreciation. "Hazel told Mabel that they offered to have Kelsey live with them after she graduated from high school last year. Said she'd be nearer to more theaters and acting opportunities. Hazel said she and George thought Kelsey was running with a rough crowd, so the invitation was also to get her involved with a better set of friends. Doe refused. Said it was okay for her daughter to visit often, which she was doing, but Doe didn't want to burden the older couple."

Beryl shrugged. "Seems logical enough. An eighteen- or nineteen-year-old could be wearing on a couple in their seventies. It's not like Kelsey would have been a big help around the house, either. Doe has spoiled that child rotten. It's a shame she won't cut the apron strings and let the young woman grow up." Beryl realized she was getting off the subject. She stopped to take a deep breath and asked with more than a hint of impatience, "Did Mabel tell you anything that struck you as being out of the ordinary?"

Nadine frowned, thinking over the conversation she'd had the night before. "There is one thing that struck me as odd. Mabel said she remembered the Bennets' son telling her that he'd been born in Chicago. She remembered because she tried to talk to Hazel about Shedd Aquarium, apparently Mabel's favorite place to visit whenever she goes to that city. Mabel said when she finally got the chance to mention the incredible diversity of marine life there, Hazel got all flustered and actually denied ever having been to Illinois, let alone its largest city. Mabel said Hazel seemed very adamant and even slightly upset that anyone would ask her about Chicago."

"Hmmm," Beryl said, raising her coffee cup to

take a sip and made no other comment.

"That's it, I'm afraid." Nadine searched her friend's face for even a glimmer of pleasure over the tidbit. When she detected none, her heart sank. "Now that I think about it, it doesn't sound all that significant. Does it to you?" She felt she'd accomplished nothing whatsoever. Maybe she wasn't such a good investigative partner, after all.

"Hard to say," Beryl replied. "What else happened? You haven't yet told me how you got the tumbler."

Nadine's spirits rose a little. She really had been pleased with her cleverness and hoped to impress her more experienced friend. "The three of us were outside for only half an hour or so before Mabel said she was getting cold and wanted to go in. She'd really said all she was going to and, as you now know, it was nothing startling. I don't think Henry learned anything new about the Bennets, either. At any rate, he seemed disappointed. Mabel does try to be important, doesn't she." Nadine said rhetorically.

"The glass," Beryl prompted.

"Oh … right." Nadine went back to the subject. "We had just gotten up to go back into the dining room when Clara appeared. I swear, she materialized from thin air. I even wondered if she'd been spying on us and trying to eavesdrop. I bet she saw us get up and didn't want to lose the chance to snag Henry."

"Were you surprised? From what I understand, if Henry's around, Clara can't be far away," Beryl said.

"I hadn't been thinking about her, one way or the other," Nadine said, "but it was great good fortune that she did show up. She always has some excuse for pulling him away from other people … or other women, I should say," Nadine added with a grin. "Last night, she asked him to lend her his arm for a walk in the gorgeous night air … so she wouldn't trip on those impractical shoes she's always wearing."

Nadine wrinkled her nose with the description, then brightened again as she thought of her coup. "I told Henry to go ahead and I'd return the tray and our glasses. When we were inside, I told Mabel to go grab the elevator, that I'd swing by the service counter where we leave cups and glasses for the after-hours staff and be right along. I've always kept one of Ralph's hankies in my tote, even when he was alive. That's what gave me the idea in the first place. I guess I do watch too much television because I thought of all those shows where the detective picks up something with the perp's fingerprints on it, and it's nearly always a glass." Nadine made a sweeping hand gesture toward the object on the counter. "And voila … here you have it."

"I don't care how much TV you watch," Beryl said, patting Nadine's shoulder. "You're a genius. I'll pass this along to Butch and see what he can find out. If you can't learn anything about Henry from the residents at the Big House, maybe his fingerprints will tell us a story." Beryl raised her eyebrows and paused a beat or two before saying, "Would you like to hear my news now?"

Sensing a big moment and seeing the gleam in her friend's eye, Nadine chuckled. "I can tell it's something good."

"I got my coat back," Beryl blurted.

"No way," Nadine exclaimed. "Where did you

find it? Was it in Hazel's house?"

"Actually, I found it in a suitcase belonging to Kelsey," Beryl said, turning serious. "There's more to the story, so before I explain, I want to show you something." She reached for the tiny plastic baggie at the end of the counter into which she'd placed the capsules that had fallen out of Kelsey's makeup case. She still was keeping her discovery of the earring to herself for the time being, but she was curious about the medicine. "Do you know what these are?"

Taking the small bag from Beryl, Nadine took only a quick glance before her heart skipped a beat. She looked up from the medication, puzzled and feeling slightly queasy as recognition dawned. Wondering if Beryl were testing her, she answered as if posing another question, "hydrochlorothiazide?"

"What's that?" Beryl asked, clearly mystified.

When Nadine realized that Beryl hadn't known, but was genuinely asking her opinion, she explained how she was able to recognize the capsule. "It's a diuretic. Ralph took it for high blood pressure. That's the generic name of the drug. Where did you get these?"

After Beryl filled her in on the upturned suitcase, the discovery of the coat, Kelsey's surprise visit and the spilled cosmetics pouch, Nadine said, "I can't imagine a young woman like Kelsey taking blood pressure medication, can you?"

Beryl slowly shook her head as she mentally went through the members of the Bennet family. "Steven was the only one I know of who had heart problems. George was an insulin-dependent diabetic, but I don't think he had particularly high blood pressure."

"Oh, no," Nadine said, feeling her throat constrict at the thought. "If George was being given insulin shots, he wouldn't have taken this. At least, he shouldn't have. The combination could be fatal. When Ralph had his heart attack, the cardiologist asked if he had any other medical conditions. The two I remember quite clearly were diabetes and gout, neither of which Ralph suffered, thank goodness."

Beryl seemed to perk up at the information. "If what you're saying is true, this might be very serious indeed." She rose abruptly and removed the breakfast dishes before pulling her laptop computer forward and lifting the lid. As she waited for the machine to boot, she explained what she was thinking. "George's death has always seemed sudden and unexpected to me. Hazel's illness was also very puzzling." At a sound from the computer, she swiveled to face the display and began to type rapidly.

Nadine was too stunned by what Beryl had said to do anything but watch her friend pound away at the keyboard.

"This is it," Beryl exclaimed after several minutes of scrolling through site after site. "This has got to be it," she repeated more emphatically. "Listen." Sliding her eyes to Nadine and quickly back to the screen, she read, "*[hydrochlorothiazide] may interact with other medicines that make you lightheaded, such as cold medicines, pain medications* ... blah, blah, blah." Her head moved slightly from side to side as she scanned down the display. "Here ... *or **insulin** or oral diabetes* *medications.*" The look she threw Nadine was one of shock and disbelief before Beryl returned to quote again. As she spoke, her voice rose with anger. "*Hydrochlorothiazide, a sulfonamide, can cause an idiosyncratic reaction, resulting in acute transient myopia and acute angle-closure glaucoma. Symptoms include acute onset of decreased visual acuity or ocular pain and typically occur within hours to weeks of drug initiation.*"

When she finished, she swiveled her chair again to face Nadine straight on. "Severe eye pain. That's what was wrong with Hazel. That's why she had to lie in a darkened room and had warm compresses over her eyes."

Chapter 19

"This is much more serious than swiping a coat. I think we've got ourselves a murder here ... maybe even two, wouldn't you say?" Beryl said to Nadine, not expecting an answer. She felt certain she was right, but realized she should call in the experts. She was experienced enough to know that simply finding the capsules in Kelsey's luggage was not sufficient proof to have her arrested, let alone charged with killing Hazel and, maybe, George.

"We need to have a powwow. I'll phone Butch." Beryl looked over her shoulder at the wall clock. "He and Cecily are probably in church, but I'll leave a message and see if he can meet us for lunch. We should include Jessica, too. The fire in Hazel's house was too much of a coincidence. I'd be willing to bet Kelsey set it purposely to destroy evidence. Can you call and see if Jessica can meet us here?"

"Of course," Nadine said and headed for the living room to fetch her phone from the tote she'd left on the chair.

While Nadine phoned Jessica, Beryl punched speed dial for the Yancys and left a message, asking Butch to call her as soon as possible. She then disappeared into her bedroom and returned with scraps of paper in her hand and a sapphire earring that comprised what she now considered additional evidence in a possible murder investigation.

Smudge followed closely on her heels, probably sensing the excitement in the air. Stooping to give the cat a perfunctory scratch beneath his jawline, Beryl returned to her chair, set the jewel to one side and placed the pieces of paper on the counter top alongside the hankie-wrapped drinking glass and the prescription capsules.

Finished with her own phone call, Nadine resumed her seat next to Beryl. "Jessica will be here at one o'clock."

Nodding acknowledgment, Beryl asked, "What do we know about the Bennets?" as she pulled her laptop to the edge of the counter.

Nadine shrugged. "That they moved here from Seattle," she mused as she picked up the library receipt. Speaking almost to herself, she said, "It's possible they came from Chicago, but then, I wonder why Hazel would deny ever having been to Illinois."

Perusing the articles of evidence, Beryl picked up the grocery list. "What do you think this tells us, if anything?"

Nadine glanced up from reading book titles and put a finger on the note Doe had left on Beryl's door, asking her to keep a look-out for Smudge. "It tells us that Doe made out the grocery list. It also tells us that she did not write the words on the back of this library receipt," Nadine continued, holding up the slip in her hand.

"I wish I knew what was in that safe." Beryl muttered as she began to type search words into her computer.

"What safe?" Nadine asked, looking up from the library receipt she'd been examining, turning it front to back to study the handwritten words as well as the printed titles.

"Joey and I found a safe in the laundry room. Didn't I mention it?" When Nadine shook her head, Beryl explained about the shelves she wanted Joey to build for her and how he'd discovered that the box at the bottom was actually a hiding place for the safe. "And here I thought all along that its purpose was to keep laundry soap off the floor in case of a water leak. It made a good shelf for Smudge's food and water bowls, too, which is what I'd use it for."

Nadine's focus stayed on the fact that the two snoops had found a safe. "Does it have one of those locks with numbers around a circle? Maybe we can get a stethoscope and listen to the tumblers," she proposed, pleased with herself for the idea. "Bet we could borrow one from the nurses at the Big House."

Beryl narrowed her eyes as she stared at her friend for a long pause. Finally, she admonished, "You really do watch too much television."

Crushed, Nadine defended herself. "What's wrong with my idea?"

The crestfallen look on her face tugged at Beryl's conscience. "Nothing, I suppose, except safes nowadays all seem to be digital. Touch pads, not dials. We have to figure out what the combination might be, and we don't even know how many numbers George might have chosen."

"What about their son's birthday? Or maybe their anniversary. Those are numbers I would try, anyway," Nadine offered.

Beryl said nothing, although she thought the idea worth considering. Both women returned to what they'd been doing and silence filled the room for several minutes before Nadine gave a sudden gasp.

"What now?" Beryl demanded, distracted from her computer searches.

"I wonder if Hazel might have been sending a message through these stories," Nadine said, her excitement growing.

Another hairbrained idea, Beryl thought but didn't say aloud. What she did say in a tone that reflected her doubt. "You mean because they're *murder* mysteries?" Raising an eyebrow, she sputtered a laugh. "We're already working on the theory that Hazel was probably killed, so perhaps you're right, but how does that saying go … 'a day late and a dollar short' or maybe 'too little, too late'? Even if she was still alive, who did she think would see her message, let alone lead anyone to her killer?"

Even if she were *still alive* … Nadine ground her teeth, but not just for the grammatical gaffe. She was also annoyed that Beryl was dismissing all of her ideas so easily. "No, wait," Nadine insisted, putting a hand on Beryl's forearm. "Listen." She raised the list and read the first title, "*Strong Poison.*" Staring hard into Beryl's eyes, she said, "I think that's significant, considering your discovery of the hydrochlorothiazide. It's conceivable that these particular books were checked out by Hazel as clues to what was happening to her."

"She couldn't have checked them out," Beryl said. "She'd been bedridden for the past month. Remember?"

"I know the lending period is three weeks and these are only recently overdue, so I get your point, but aren't you being a bit picky?" Nadine frowned but refused to be discouraged. "She could have asked Doe or Kelsey to get them for her, or even someone from the readers group." Suddenly thinking of another point, Nadine exclaimed, "You said she was suffering from eye pain, even as early on as George's funeral, so why would she want these books if not to raise some sort of suspicion? She certainly wouldn't have expected to read them." Nadine sniffed with self-satisfaction as she squinted at Beryl.

"Maybe she expected someone to read them *to* her." Beryl raised an eyebrow in a silent "answer that one" gesture. Taking the receipt from Nadine, she read the second title, *The Crime at Black Dudley*. With a slight cough to mask the sarcasm in her tone, she said, "What does that tell you … that a crime was committed?"

Nadine's face grew an alarming shade of red as she retorted, "No, Miss Smarty-Pants, it tells me that Hazel was being held against her will."

Surprised by the answer, Beryl said less facetiously, "Explain."

"In Black Dudley, house guests are held captive by a gang of thugs," Nadine retorted. "And before you poke fun of the others, *Murder Most Foul* speaks for itself, I believe. I don't know about *Scales of Justice* except that the author was also an actress and set many of her stories in theaters."

"This En-gayo person?" Beryl asked.

"The name is pronounced *Nye-o*," Nadine said, "It's a Mauri name. Ngaio Marsh was a New

Zealander. She was also an actress and a director of theater plays." Nadine paused and her eyes grew wide as realization struck her. "Hazel was pointing the finger at Kelsey. More proof that Kelsey must have murdered poor Hazel."

"Whoa," Beryl warned. "Hold on. I think you're making a lot of surmises from this list of books. You might be right, but it seems a stretch. Doe was an actress, too, you know. Before she was first married, she used to appear in local amateur productions."

Nadine was convinced she was on to something important. "What about these words in the shaky handwriting on the back? Fairly obvious that Hazel wrote *Murder*, *Frame* and *Help*? What about those?"

"What about them?" Beryl was losing patience. She thought Nadine was trying too hard to pull meaning from a bunch of books. Before her friend could argue the point, Beryl softened her opinion slightly, not wanting to totally dampen Nadine's enthusiasm, "Okay, I might grant you *Murder* and maybe even a cry for *Help*, but how does *Frame* fit into your theory? Who was being framed and for what?"

With a firm set to her jaw, Nadine muttered, "I can't think of everything. What do *you* think it means?"

Before Beryl could come up with an answer, the doorbell rang.

Cecily Yancy stood in the doorway, Butch behind her. "What's this I hear about you, girl? What have you gone and gotten yourself mixed up in?" The big grin on her face belied the scolding as Butch's wife pulled Beryl into a hug as warm as his. Cecily was as tall as Beryl and outweighed her by about 50 pounds. Beryl returned the embrace as enthusiastically as her best friend. Finally, holding Beryl at arm's length, Cecily added to the good-natured scolding. "And why haven't you called to ask my advice?"

"Butch told me you were dealing with a colicky great-grandchild," Beryl said.

"We are that," Cecile rolled her eyes. "As a matter of fact, we were on our way down the mountain to see the family when we got your message. I can talk and take care of a baby at the same time, you know. So what's your next excuse for ignoring me?"

Beryl scrunched her face into an exaggerated expression of apology. "I have nothing to say that won't further incriminate me."

Before she finished, Cecily began talking over her. "You know we always solve Butch's cases together."

Over Cicely's left shoulder, Beryl saw the look of mock horror and disbelief on Butch's face. Before his wife got too carried away with her joking, he said, "Are you going in or am I supposed to stand out here while you two yak?"

Laughing, Cicely linked her arm through Beryl's, and the trio moved into the kitchen. "Cecily and Butch, I'd like you to meet another friend," Beryl said, introducing Nadine.

"This your new partner-in-crime?" Cicely kidded, turning away from Beryl to toss a wink at Nadine.

Feeling overwhelmed in the company of three people who diminished the room, not to mention the intimidating police presence, Nadine stayed rooted to her chair and nodded her greeting.

Immediately, Cicely nodded back. "Nice to meet you, Nadine. Don't mind me. I love giving this woman a hard time whenever I can."

"Coffee?" Beryl asked, purposely changing the subject. Cicely was known to go on at length about the friendship they shared, usually embarrassing Beryl in the process.

"No, honey, but thanks. As I said, we're on our way to the kids' to help out in the guise of having Sunday dinner." Cecily gave a hearty, conspiratorial laugh before continuing. "This man of mine wanted me to sit in the car, but you know how well I obey, particularly when I haven't seen you in a dog's age." She tucked her arm through Butch's as she spoke, but her glance remained on Beryl. "I want to know what you have him running around for, and then we have to skedaddle. Tell me what's gotten you so worked up about this neighbor of yours."

Before answering, Beryl looked sideways at Nadine and explained, "Butch wouldn't dare keep this woman in the dark about any of his activities, especially the more interesting ones that involve police work." To Cicely, she said with a tone of annoyance, "It began when someone switched coats on me, *someone* who turned out to be staying next door, however temporarily. Then, my neighbor dies unexpectedly and someone tries to burn down her house, uncomfortably close to my own."

Cicely jumped in as Beryl took a breath. "Okay, okay. You and I have snooped together enough around this man's cases that I get your drift." She flashed a brilliant smile at her husband before turning back to Beryl. "So, what do you need from us?"

Beryl looked at Butch. "Would you mind running some fingerprints for me?"

"Would it matter if I did?" Butch said, feigning a scowl.

"Not a bit," Cecily answered for him with a twinkle in her eye. "Whose prints?"

"I'd rather not say until the results are in, if you don't mind," Beryl answered. "Wouldn't want to harm anyone's reputation." She paused to slide her eyes toward Nadine before adding, "And I'd like to know what name you come up with, on the off chance this person isn't who he says he is."

Cecily looked at her husband with mock seriousness. "Well, detective, at least we know it's a man," she said solemnly.

Beryl raised her eyes toward the ceiling for an instant. "I'll get a paper sack so you won't contaminate my evidence," she said, pulling out a drawer to retrieve a small brown bag. She then folded the corners of Roger's handkerchief carefully into the glass and put the bundle into the sack. "Then there's this," she said, holding up a snack-sized plastic baggie into which she'd put one of the prescription capsules. "If you could give this to the coroner … it might be what killed Hazel and possibly George." She added the medication to the paper bag before folding down the top and handing it to Butch. "Finally," she picked up the sapphire earring and extended it in her palm so both Yancys could see it. "What do you think of this?"

With a low whistle, Cecily picked up the piece of jewelry and held it up toward the light. "Beautiful," she breathed. "And expensive," she said in a graver voice.

"That's just the thing," Beryl said and told them about it in the coat pocket. "I can't believe something this valuable was left in a coat in a theater's wardrobe collection. I think it belongs to Kelsey and why she wanted the old coat back. What doesn't sit right with me is that she owns something this expensive."

"Very nice," Butch said, accepting the piece of jewelry from his wife. "Are you sure she doesn't have this kind of money?"

Beryl took back the earring and said, "I think the mother might, but I doubt if the daughter does. If it really is hers, why didn't she just ask me if I'd found it?"

"Do you want me to beat the truth out of her," Butch said, keeping a straight face.

With a laugh, Beryl put her arms out and gave Butch a hug. "I know you two are my best friends and would do anything for me, but let's wait on the torture, shall we?"

Snickering, Cecily agreed before tugging on her husband's arm. "Now you have your assignment, we'd better go. I promised to help with the cooking." She turned to Nadine. "Pleasure meeting you. Have Beryl bring you up to visit sometime soon, will you do that? Georgetown is especially beautiful in the fall, I think, and I love showing people its history."

Nadine smiled. "I'd like that very much. I haven't been there in years, and never with my own tour guide."

The comment earned a gentle goodbye hug from Cicely before she wrapped her arms around Beryl. "Don't be such a stranger. I've missed you."

As he followed his wife to the door, Butch held up the bag. "I'll see what I can do. Might take a few days."

Chapter 20

"It's nice you could stay such good friends all these years," Nadine observed when Beryl reappeared after seeing off the Yancys.

Beryl nodded, feeling the warmth Cicely always left her. "I don't know what I'd have done without their support after Michael died. We lived only a block apart when Butch was still full-time on the force. I think I spent more time in Cicely's kitchen than in my own, and her kids were in and out of my house all the time."

"How many children do they have?" Nadine asked.

"Five ... or four now," Beryl corrected as the light disappeared from her face. "They lost a son in Afghanistan. Their middle kid, a daughter, is a nurse, stationed at Fort Irwin, so she gets home a couple of times a year. The other three live here, plus there are eight grandchildren and one great with another great on the way." Beryl's grin returned as she fell silent, thinking of the boisterous family with hearts as big as their patriarch's.

Almost instantly, the mood seemed to dissolve and her face clouded again. Beryl sunk to her chair at the low kitchen counter and put her face in her hands.

"What is it? What's wrong?" Nadine immediately leapt to her feet and put an arm around her friend's shoulders.

Beryl slowly shook her head. "I just need a minute." Several seconds passed before, rubbing fingers down her cheeks, she rose and went to the stove. Moving mechanically, she filled the kettle and put it on to boil while she grabbed a teapot and dropped in several tea bags.

"Are you going to tell me what's on you mind?" Nadine finally broke the silence.

"I think this whole affair just got to me," Beryl said with a wan smile. "Arsonists, prowlers and murderers. And everything seems so muddled. We've got bits of paper that seem related, but not. There's that expensive earring in the pocket of an old, decrepit coat. If Hazel was taking medication that was causing her severe pain, was it willingly? Why does Kelsey have blood pressure medication? Why didn't Doe put Hazel in a hospital or in the skilled-nursing facility at Sunnydale?" Beryl shook her head. "I could go on, but suddenly I feel like I'm spinning my wheels, running in place and getting nowhere."

"I know what you mean. I've been feeling quite confused myself, but I was hoping you'd be able to help clear things up for me," Nadine confessed.

Beryl turned and looked at her friend as if she were seeing her for the first time. After a long pause, she began to laugh. The more she laughed, the harder it became to stop. Her amusement was infectious and Nadine's chuckle turned into a rollicking belly-laugh. Tears were running down their faces by the time the whistle blasting from the kettle brought them to their senses.

"What was that all about?" Nadine asked, grabbing a tissue from the box on the counter and dabbing her eyes.

"Hysterics, probably," Beryl replied, swallowing another chuckle. She brought the filled teapot to the counter, plucked out a tissue for herself and went back to the cupboard for cups. Finally settled in her chair, she patted Nadine's knee and said, "but it felt good."

The two gulped down sniggers as Beryl poured them each a mug of tea and passed an open bag of cookies toward Nadine. "Help yourself," she offered, unceremoniously. "We've got to organize our thoughts." Taking a sip before putting her cup aside, she spread out the various items they'd been collecting over the past few days.

"First, there are the scraps from the pocket of that coat," Nadine began.

"Right," Beryl said, her attention on lining up the items in question. "A library receipt, the grocery list, fast food ticket and three candy wrappers. There's also this unmatched earring that I found yesterday after giving the coat a more thorough search."

"Another discovery was the note that Doe left on your door, leading to the conclusion that she wrote the grocery list which further convinced us that the coat belonged to her."

"Or to her daughter," Beryl corrected. "Which is what we now know for certain."

"Right," Nadine agreed. Watching Beryl smooth out the library ticket, she said, "I wonder if the books were ever returned." Frowning at Beryl, she continued her train of thought, "And who checked them out, if Hazel was bedridden? Surely she couldn't have made it over to the library herself."

"I'll ask Doe," Beryl said, sliding the fast food receipt between the grocery list and the library ticket. "She must know, having been Hazel's main caregiver for the past month." She arranged the candy wrappers in a pile. "Do you suppose these have any significance at all?" Adding them to the stack, she glanced at Nadine. "I've been keeping them with the rest because all these bits of paper seem to go together. I can't explain it, but I feel these have as much meaning as the rest, maybe more so."

"Whether they do or not," Nadine said, watching Beryl's hands, "I think you're correct to keep everything together until this mystery is solved." She sounded supportive but doubtful as to the importance of the red and gold foil.

"What else have we got," Beryl said rhetorically, bringing forth the last of their findings. "Why would Kelsey Martine be carrying around a blood pressure medication?"

Instead of answering, Nadine picked up her mug of tea and sipped absently before cringing at the tepid liquid and quickly putting her cup aside. At that moment, the doorbell rang.

Noting the time on the stove clock as she left the kitchen, Beryl wondered who would be calling at 11:12. She wasn't expecting a delivery. "You're early," she said, opening the door to find Jessica on the stoop.

The young woman nodded as she stepped into the

hall. "I can't stay long. I'm meeting a couple of the guys at Red Rocks. We're running the amphitheater this afternoon. It's been a quiet day, so Captain said I could take off." Jessica said, accepting a brief hug from Nadine who'd risen to greet the young firefighter.

"Running the amphitheater?" she questioned.

Jessica smiled down at her former teacher. "We run up and down the steps to train for our firefighter's annual physical ability test."

"A what?" Beryl asked. She'd gone out briefly to check the day's temperature and had missed part of the conversation as she'd stepped back in and shut the door.

"Our physical ability test," Jessica repeated. "We have to pass the PAT each year to keep our jobs."

"Every year?" Nadine asked, eyes widening in amazement."

"And whenever we've been away from the job for any length of time," Jessica explained. "Lives depend on our keeping in shape … not just ourselves and the rest of the crew, but victims, too," she added.

"Running up and down steps helps you do that?" Nadine asked. She was still a bit puzzled at the picture.

"Yes, it builds stamina. After that, we'll hit the gym for weights and the rest of the workout," she said.

"More workouts?" Nadine was impressed with the stamina and dedication of her former student.

"Makes sense that you keep in shape," Beryl opined. "Wish it had been a requirement for Michael's fellow cops. My husband and Butch kept in good shape. They were always competing with each other at the gym, but some of the officers they worked with would probably have dropped dead from a heart attack if they had to run around the block."

"What sort of things do you do," Nadine asked Jessica.

"The short version is that we have to simulate eight job-related activities like charged line advance, equipment carry, forcible entry, ceiling breach and pull, ladder heel and raise, stair climb and victim rescue … all in full gear while carrying a fifty-pound weight on our backs. We're timed," she added, rolling her eyes. "It's seven minutes of pure hell."

"When is this test?" Nadine, ever the teacher, wanted to know.

"The captain's nice enough to test us when the weather's apt to be cooler. I expect we'll be recertifying in late October or early November." Jessica grimaced. "I haven't been to the gym in a while, so I've got some catching up to do if I'm going to pass this year."

"Are the men given the same test?" Nadine wondered aloud.

"You mean do I get special privileges because I'm a woman?" Jessica shook her head with a frown. "No way. We all depend on each other in a crisis. Women on the crews have to be as fit and as capable as the men."

"Why are we standing here at the front door?" Beryl said. "You may be in shape, but I need to sit down. Besides, I'm getting tired just listening to all you have to do," she added with a smile.

Jessica grinned and looked at her watch. "I only stopped by because you asked me to, but I can't stay long. The guys will be waiting."

"Just for a minute then," Beryl urged. With a hand on the young woman's forearm, she drew her toward the kitchen. Heading for the chairs at the low counter, she saw Smudge sitting beside her coffee cup, batting at the candy wrappers. "Here," she scolded, advancing on the cat. "You know you're not allowed up there. What do you think you're doing?"

Too late, Smudge shoved one of the papers onto the floor and leaned over to watch it fall.

Jessica bent to retrieve it, and Smudge immediately batted it off. Laughing, she dutifully picked it up and said, "He reminds me of my little nephew, always throwing something on the floor when he sees me. He knows I'll hand it back so he can promptly drop it on the floor again." She scrunched up her nose at Nadine. "Is it me or do little kids play 'pick up' with everyone?"

Nadine laughed. "I think all children and pets go through a 'retrieve' stage. It was one of my Ralph's favorite games as a toddler."

"Stop that," Beryl said when Smudge patted the paper to the edge of the counter and watched as it floated to the floor. This time, after she recovered it, she shooed the cat off the table. "That's enough. Go to your room," she commanded and was amazed to see him slink off toward the bedroom, flicking the tip of his tail.

"Well trained," Nadine commented with a chuckle.

Jessica rested a thigh against the low partition and

idly picked up another of the candy wrappers. "Yummm," she murmured, "chocolate-covered cherries. These were one of my mother's favorites."

"Is that what these foils are?" Beryl asked. She held out her hand for Jessica's wrapper and carefully placed it back on the pile. "They were in the pocket of that coat we told you about. Turns out, it belongs to Kelsey. Well, not exactly hers," Beryl amended. "She 'sort of borrowed it' … her words … from a theater in Calgary where she was auditioning. Said it was cold and she needed it."

"How'd you find that out?" Jessica said, shaking her head in disapproval.

Nadine spoke up. "Beryl and I have learned a bit since we saw you last. Sit and let us fill you in. That's why we wanted you here, in case you can add something we might have overlooked." She motioned Jessica to the chair Nadine had occupied earlier before turning to Beryl. "If you don't mind my puttering in your kitchen, I'll make tea and sandwiches while you fill Jessica in on your adventure. My obtaining Henry's fingerprints is minor compared to what you've discovered."

"Putter away," Beryl replied. Resuming her own seat at the counter, she told Jessica about meeting Joey and going into Hazel's house after receiving permission from both Sunnydale's director and Doe Bennet. Breezing over the house search, Beryl told of finding her coat in Kelsey's suitcase just as the young woman herself walked into the bedroom. That explanation led to the discovery of the prescription drugs and Nadine's identification. "So, it looks suspiciously like Kelsey might have murdered her step-grandmother, but we have no actual proof," Beryl concluded.

"Wow, that's quite a story," Jessica said, her eyes wide. "What do you think I can do to help?"

"Can you get us a copy of the report on the fire in Hazel's bedroom?" Beryl asked. "It'll be public record, but I'm guessing you can get it quicker than us."

"She needs to *get a copy*, not *get us*," Nadine qualified, placing a plate of ham and cheese sandwiches on the counter. "And she can get it 'quicker than we.'" She called over her shoulder as she went back for the teapot.

Beryl turned and stared silently after her friend.

"The noun that follows the verb is its object," Nadine explained, returning to place the teapot on the counter. "And, if you add a verb to the subject of your qualifying phrase, she can get the copy 'quicker than we can'."

Beryl stared.

Noticing the hostile look on her friend's face, Nadine hurriedly said, "Sorry." She neither sounded nor looked apologetic as she winked at Jessica. "Habit."

Hiding a smile, Jessica examined the sandwiches, then glanced at her watch. "I shouldn't eat anything before training," she said, rising. "I'll get you whatever I can find on the fire," she said to Beryl, waving her down when she began to rise. "I can show myself out." Turning to Nadine, she gave her old teacher a hug. "I'll call when I have something."

After the front door closed and Nadine was seated, she turned to Beryl and pouted. "I didn't get to tell her about my fingerprints," she wailed.

"It's okay. You can tell her later," Beryl said, choosing a sandwich from the plate. "Eat up. We have a house to pack up and a memorial service to plan."

Chapter 21

Finished with lunch, Beryl took Nadine to Hazel's, noticing on the way over that Joey had taken down the board covering the bedroom window. She wondered when someone would get around to replacing the glass. For now, she'd have to settle for the hole in the wall to air out the place a little, but she had no illusions that the foul odors would be gone before a complete repainting and re-carpeting was done.

She'd told Nadine about shutting the door the previous evening and warned her that the smelly room was where they needed to concentrate their efforts that afternoon. When they entered, the air was damp and as stinky as Beryl had feared. Opening the bedroom to the outside had helped, but since the sun hadn't yet penetrated, the room was cold.

"I'd like to get that mattress out of here," Beryl said as the two stood in the doorway, taking in the mess. "It might improve the smell in here. Give me a hand, will you?"

Nadine grabbed hold of the bottom left-hand corner while Beryl took the top. Together they tugged and pulled, grunting and groaning, until the queen-size cushion was all but completely off the box springs. Dropping their side to the floor left only a foot between it and the dresser drawers. The night table would also be difficult to search with the sodden mattress in the way, but Beryl figured, if she had to, she could lean in from the side to search the one small drawer.

"I need to call Joey and have him come get this out of here," she said after a minute of frowning at the narrow passage they'd just created. Nadine might not have a problem working in a space that tiny, but Beryl didn't want to trip and fall back onto that wet and blackened mess.

"No phone in here," Nadine observed, standing at the end of the bed. "Doe must have removed it so Hazel wouldn't be bothered by the ringing."

"Or so nobody could speak to Hazel without Doe knowing about it," Beryl grumbled half to herself.

Ignoring the remark, Nadine reminded her friend that it was Sunday. "Would he be working today?"

"Joey's always working," Beryl said, speaking with confidence.

Uncertain of her friend's actual knowledge, Nadine said, "I saw a wall phone in the kitchen. You seem to be hemmed in over there by the window. Do you want me to call the receptionist at the Big House and see if Joey's available?"

"Do you know him? Has he done work around your apartment?" Beryl asked.

"We haven't even been introduced," Nadine replied with a frown. "Does that matter?"

"It might," Beryl said. "I'd better be the one to call the main desk. They'll track him down and, even if he's busy, Joey won't put me off." She brightened slightly at the thought of her adoring fan. *Who would have guessed a devoted handyman would be one of the perks of having married a police officer?* she thought before mentally shaking herself back to the task at hand. As she inched her way down the path between the bureau and mattress, sliding a hand along the dresser to keep her balance, she spoke her next thought aloud. "Let's hope Doe hasn't contacted the phone company to discontinue service."

In the kitchen, Beryl was in luck. Not only did she get a dial tone, but when she reached the receptionist at the Big House, Joey was in the lobby and came directly to the phone.

"Hi, Beryl," he answered in his cheery voice. "What can I do you for?"

"Will you come get the mattress out of Hazel's bedroom? I want to go through the room this afternoon and the darn thing is in the way. Maybe you can drag it out to the patio until the trash pickup this week."

"Can't right now," he replied with a tone of sincere regret. "I was just on my way to the weight room. I've got a session with Henry, and I'm already late."

Beryl had expected that Joey would drop whatever he was doing and show up at Hazel's immediately, so she didn't respond while she wondered how she might rearrange her plans for the afternoon. One thing was certain … she wouldn't work in the room with the mattress in the middle of the floor.

Probably mistaking her silence for disapproval, Joey broke the silence. "Look, I can be there in an hour. I'm sure if I ask Henry, he'll help, but I doubt he'll put off his regular workout."

Beryl didn't feel like hanging around that long, twiddling her thumbs. "Guess that'll be okay," she replied with some reluctance. "Nadine and I have other things to do, so we won't wait for you. You can get in with the master key, can't you?" Then, remembering the window, she snickered. "Or you can climb in through the hole in the wall."

Joey didn't react to her humor. He simply said, "Gotta go. See you later."

Back in the bedroom, Nadine was standing on the far side of the box springs. "Look what I found," she said, holding up what looked like a large, colorful marble in the palm of her hand.

"What is it?" Beryl stopped at the foot of the bed and leaned to get a closer look.

"It's one of those chocolate-covered cherries that Jessica mentioned. It's wrapped in the same red and gold foil you found in your coat's pocket," Nadine said as her eyes widened with wonder.

"Not *my* coat," Beryl reminded her friend unnecessarily.

"Whatever." Nadine rolled her eyes before continuing. "I found this on the box springs. It must have been under the mattress. It's a little squished, but it doesn't look like the heat got to it."

"Why would Hazel put candy under the mattress?" Beryl asked, nearly laughing at the absurdity before realizing how ill the woman must have been to do such a thing. Taking the candy from Hazel, Beryl examined it more closely. "Whatever Hazel's reason, this is just more proof that the coat came from this house." She glanced once more around the room before catching Hazel's eye and, with a slight jerk of her head, motioned toward the door behind her. "Let's get out of here. We'll pack up Hazel's things after Joey gets rid of this mattress."

Once again in Beryl's kitchen, Nadine asked, "Shall we start planning the memorial service?"

Preoccupied with making a mental list of tasks that needed to be done, Beryl shook her head, then began to share her thoughts. "I've got to get some cardboard boxes and large trash bags before we can pack up next door. I might as well check out the liquor stores and groceries while we wait for Joey. They always have empty cartons they're wanting to get rid of."

"Do you want me to help?" Nadine offered, biting her tongue over the sentence structure.

Beryl shook her head. "Not at the moment, but tell you what … we're going to need information for the memorial service. Why don't you check with the book club members and find out all you can about Hazel? You know, like what you told me before about her being a librarian before she moved to Sunnydale."

Nadine looked skeptical. "From Clara's attitude at the meeting the other day, I don't expect I'll get much in the way of positive comments from her or from her two ladies-in-waiting." Remembering the woman who had arrived with the walker, Nadine brightened. "There was one woman from assisted living, though. She seemed fond of Hazel. I think her name was Irene or Ingrid or I-something." Shaking her head as if trying to bring the name to mind, Nadine straightened her spine with renewed purpose.

"Whatever her name is, I'll find her and report back later this afternoon."

Chapter 22

Stepping out of Beryl's house onto the patio, Nadine looked across at the Bennets' bungalow. *It'll soon belong to someone else.* The thought came unbidden to her mind. Why was she feeling so depressed? After all, she'd never even met the pair. Shortly after she'd moved to Sunnydale, George was buried and Hazel bedridden. Nadine supposed her distress was due to being in Hazel's bedroom. That's when Nadine's stomach had begun to sour. She could tell the room had been attractive with lovely floral-print curtains and a quilt to match. All blackened and water stained now, smelling of burned fabrics. *Who would have started a fire*, she wondered, *and why?*

Approaching the Big House, she forced her thoughts to the task ahead. *Imagine the woman in the frame on Beryl's kitchen counter*, she told herself. That woman and her husband should have the best sendoff Beryl and she could arrange. Nadine continued her mental pep talk as she entered Sunnydale's main lobby. She cast her eyes downward as she crossed the vestibule, hoping to discourage anyone who might motion her over for a chat. She didn't like to appear unfriendly, but neither did she want to get waylaid by someone who might talk her ear off. Nadine had a mission and she didn't intend to be interrupted. She avoided the elevator and hurried to the stairwell for the same reasons.

On the second floor, Nadine turned toward the assisted living quarters, hoping to find someone who could tell her which apartment was Imogene's. *That was it*, Nadine congratulated herself silently. *Imogene. The reading club member's name was Imogene.* Fortunately, at that moment, a white-haired man in an automated wheelchair came buzzing around the corner.

"Watch out," he cried, aiming his chair at her. "I'm not responsible for what this gol durned machine does." Despite the words, he managed to stop at least six inches from Nadine's toes. "Out of my way, woman," he grumbled, "I'm on my way to bingo."

Nadine held in her laughter. She had a feeling he enjoyed playing "grumpy old man," so she stayed in his path and asked, "Do you know which apartment belongs to Imogene?"

"Imogene who?" he asked, scowling up at Nadine.

"I'm sorry, but I don't remember her last name. I only met her a couple of days ago at a book club meeting."

"Two-oh-six," the man said, angling his chair around Nadine. *So he does know how to maneuver the thing*, she thought just as he rolled away and called over his shoulder. "Only one Imogene lives here."

Nadine thought she heard him cackle as she turned to walk down the corridor, glancing at the numbers beside each door. The name plate above the numbers at 206 read *Imogene Parsons*. Happy to be reminded of her new acquaintance's last name, Nadine knocked. When she waited what seemed to be a very long time, she knocked again and bent to put an ear close to the door, listening for approaching footsteps. Hearing none, she was about to turn away when the lever dipped and a face appeared in the widening crack.

"Who is it?" Imogene asked before she'd gotten the door fully open. She was backing away, allowing room for the small-base quad cane upon which she leaned. When her eyes met Nadine's, Imogene's face brightened. "Oh, it's you. Nadine, isn't it? I remember because it's not a common name, but so pretty."

"Yes," Nadine was unexpectedly pleased by the woman's memory and compliment. "Imogene," she began, "I wonder if you have a few minutes to visit."

"Of course." The woman backed away a couple more steps, turning back into the room as she said, "Come in, come in."

Nadine entered, closing the door behind her. "I hope I'm not inconveniencing you?"

"Not at all," Imogene said with enthusiasm. She'd reached the middle of the room and turned to smile at Nadine. "Today's a good day. I don't need my walker," she explained, gently pounding the cane on the carpet several times before waving her free hand at the sparsely furnished living quarters. "Please make yourself comfortable. Seating is limited, as you can see, but I find it easier to get around with my walker and cane when a room is less cluttered." The apology was stated matter-of-factly, without remorse. "Shall I make some tea? Can you stay awhile?"

"Tea would be nice," Nadine answered, "but please let me help."

The kitchen was arranged along the near wall of the wide room. Boiling water and preparing the teapot while Imogene arranged a selection of cookies on a china plate, Nadine made small talk, admiring the home decorated in red, white and pearl gray. She exclaimed over the hot pads and matching dish towel emblazoned with red-combed roosters and fat white hens, and confessed to having the same kitchen accessories as well as the matching salt and pepper shakers.

"You must come up to my place sometime," she invited when she added the teapot to a tray with cups and saucers before following Imogene toward the plush red sofa at the opposite side of the room. An enormous painting of poinsettia blooms took up most of the white wall behind the couch. An open door to her left showed Nadine the bedroom painted in pearl gray. She guessed the bathroom was located off the sleeping chamber and thought the living space was efficiently designed. When she'd met Imogene at the book club, Nadine's initial impression of the woman had been positive. That opinion improved even more in the classy and modern surrounds. Imogene was not an invalid to be pitied, but a person with a vibrant mind and joy of life whose body was betraying her.

At the moment, Nadine's host was maintaining the social chitchat while they both had a cookie with the first sips of tea. Finally, a lull in the conversation allowed Nadine to state her purpose.

"I've actually come on a mission," she began, putting her cup and saucer on the glass-topped coffee table and shifting on the couch they shared to face Imogene more directly. "The Bennets' neighbor is putting together a memorial service for George and Hazel, and she's asked me to help. I never met either of the Bennets, so I'm at a bit of a loss. I'm hoping you can tell me some things we can use for their eulogy. When you and I spoke at the book club, I got the impression you knew Hazel quite well." Nadine didn't really know how well the two women knew each other, but she didn't think a small exaggeration was out of line.

"I did get to know her fairly well, I suppose," Imogene replied, leaning forward to slide her own saucer onto the table. "We had experiences in common, so we generally visited for a short time after each meeting. We were both librarians in our former lives, you see." The woman's smile seemed sad. "Our talks were brief, but I enjoyed them. I was so sorry to miss her husband's funeral, but it was one of my bad days. That's why I made a special effort to see her a few days later and to get her the books she wanted from the library."

Nadine's heart skipped a beat. "You checked books out for Hazel?" She wanted to make certain she understood Imogene perfectly, so Nadine asked specifically, "From Sunnydale's library?"

"Oh, no, dear. There were some mysteries she particularly wanted and asked me if I'd mind getting them from the branch in town. That was another thing we had in common … both of us enjoyed reading mysteries, especially the older ones that weren't as violent or grisly as many today."

Nadine repeated the titles she'd been puzzling over on the library receipt for the past few days.

"Yes, dear, those are the ones," Imogene confirmed.

"And you checked them out using her library card?" Again, Nadine wanted to make quite sure of her facts.

Imogene seemed slightly embarrassed when she said, "I don't have a card. I'm not able to get out as often as I'd like. When I do make an excursion, I try to make the most of my time away." She brightened a little, adding, "There's quite a good selection of titles here at Sunnydale, so I don't feel deprived."

"And you said Hazel asked particularly for those titles?" Nadine repeated.

"Oh, yes, she was very definite about those four. Didn't want anything else. No substitutes." Imogene looked curiously at Nadine. "Why do you ask? You make it sound important."

"I know this must seem strange, but I've been wondering if the titles or the plots may have had any sort of special meaning," Nadine said. "Did she happen to mention any significance or reason for her choices?"

Imogene's brow creased and she took several seconds before answering. "It's funny you should say that. When she asked if I could get the books from the library, I got the impression she wanted to explain, but her daughter-in-law kept fussing with Hazel's pillow and rearranging things on the bedside table. I know she was very caring toward Hazel, but I found her rather annoying."

"So you weren't alone with Hazel?" Nadine asked.

"Not for a second," Imogene responded with a hint of anger in her tone. "The nurse attendant who escorted me to the bungalow had the courtesy to stay in the living room, but that daughter-in-law never took the hints."

"Like what?" Nadine was curious.

"Hazel asked if she'd make some tea, but Doris … is that her name?" Imogene stopped to ask.

"Doe," Nadine corrected.

"Yes, Doe." Imogene nodded. "Well, Doe said they were fresh out of tea." Imogene made a sour face. "I ask you, who runs out of tea?"

Nadine nodded her agreement. "Nobody who drinks it on a regular basis, I imagine."

Seemingly satisfied with the support of her guest, Imogene continued her diatribe. "Hazel asked to have her wash cloth changed. The daughter-in-law said she was doing laundry and would get a fresh cloth when the clothes were done. I tell you, every attempt Hazel made to try and get that woman out of the room was put aside with a weak excuse. I got the impression Doe thought the two of us might conspire against her if she left the room."

"Yes, that does seem like very strange behavior, indeed," Nadine agreed. Thinking she'd about exhausted the questions she had about the titles, she changed the subject. "Did Hazel ask for anything besides the books?"

"No," Imogene replied after a moment's thought. Suddenly, her eyes twinkled and she smiled conspiratorially. "She was very fond of mysteries.

Will these ones be woven into the memorial service somehow?"

Nadine felt the warmth of color spread over her cheeks. "I don't know." She didn't want to upset Hazel's friend with information that was incomplete and, so far, inconclusive, so Nadine bent the truth just a little. "I found a library receipt for those books, so when you mentioned going to the library for Hazel, I wanted to be thorough. Once we have as much information as we can gather, we'll decide what to include," she ended lamely. Hoping to change the subject, she hurried on. "Did you bring Hazel anything else? A gift, perhaps?"

"No. Why? Did you find something else that puzzled you?" Imogene frowned, obviously perplexed.

Nadine raised a shoulder to show her uncertainty. "Something weird happened this afternoon that just popped into my head. I'm hoping you can clarify it for me." Nadine hesitated, wondering, not for the first time, if the discovery really mattered. She had a funny feeling that it did.

"I found a chocolate-covered cherry in her bedroom when I was helping sort through the house. They're fancy enough candies that I think it was probably a gift." Nadine hoped she wouldn't have to go into detail, but she wanted to understand why the candy had been hidden under the mattress and how the same candy wrappers might have ended up in the old swapped coat. Perhaps, if she found the gift-giver, they could throw some light on the oddity.

Imogene looked puzzled, then amused as if a memory had surfaced. She gave a short laugh. "It probably came from a box Clara took to Hazel. It's only a guess, mind you, but I bet the only reason that woman paid Hazel a visit was to find out about her relationship with Henry."

"Clara?" Nadine couldn't help her surprise. "Clara took chocolates to Hazel?"

Imogene nodded. "That old woman can't stand to be without a man. She has her sights set on Henry and woe be to anybody who stands in her way." Imogene must have seen the shock on Nadine's face because she went on to explain, "Henry took a box of those chocolates to the Bennets when he moved to Sunnydale. He'd do that periodically … pick someone out and take them flowers or candy. His way of getting to know folks, I guess." Imogene shrugged.

"Does he visit you?" Nadine was thinking she had done Henry an injustice, assuming he had ulterior motives when he was simply an outgoing, friendly guy. "Is that how you know about the cherries?"

Imogene chuckled. "Oh, no. I don't know Henry much at all. Hazel mentioned the candy at our club meeting the following day. Henry had joined us that day, so Hazel thanked him and asked how he knew the candies were their favorites. She confided to me later that George wouldn't be able to share them with her, being diabetic and all. A shame really."

Nadine assumed the "shame" was George's condition and not the fact that he couldn't share the treat. She returned her attention to what Imogene was saying when the woman continued to explain. "A few days after George's funeral, when we learned Hazel was ill, Clara told the group that she would take a box of those same chocolate-covered cherries to Hazel from all of us." When Nadine didn't respond, Imogene added, "Don't you see? Clara only wanted to check out the competition. She was not a particular pal of Hazel's. It might be mean of me to say, but that gift was more about curiosity than condolences."

Nadine was thinking of the candy she'd discovered on top of the box springs and wondered again why Hazel would want to hide the chocolate under her mattress. Hoping to avoid a catty chat about the book club hostess that would get them off the subject uppermost on her mind, Nadine asked, "Was Henry a close friend of the Bennets?" When Imogene frowned slightly at the question, Nadine quickly added, "I heard that George and Hazel were somewhat reclusive, so how did Henry know their favorite candy?"

Imogene tipped her head in thought. After a brief pause, she shook her head. "Actually, I got the impression Henry was surprised when Hazel mentioned the fact, but he didn't want to admit that it was purely an accident." Imogene gave another short laugh. "Henry might have bought them because they were his own favorites. Or," she chuckled again, "he might have received them as a gift and simply passed them along because he didn't want to eat them. You know how proud he is of his physique. He's so proud of the fact that he weighs the same as he did in his twenties, he doesn't realize that what used to be in his chest has sagged to his waist."

Both women laughed at that, and the conversation turned to a few more tidbits of information Imogene remembered Hazel having mentioned. When Nadine finally took her leave, Imogene slowly walked her to the door.

Stepping into the hall after thanking her host profusely, Nadine thought of one more question. "Did Hazel ever mention where she and George lived before moving to Sunnydale?"

Imogene nodded. "They came here from Seattle."

"She never mentioned Chicago?" Nadine wanted to know.

"No, dear. I would have remembered that. I'm from Chicago myself."

Chapter 23

The next few days Beryl spent packing up George and Hazel's personal belongings. Nadine put in some long hours, helping out when she wasn't gathering information on the couple. She was puzzled about the rumor that the Bennets had been living in Chicago when their son Steven was born. Beryl had no idea how the gossip began, but she had also been under the impression that the family had come from Chicago. Whether or not that piece of information was significant, she didn't know, but it did seem odd that Hazel would deny the association so vehemently.

Beryl shrugged it off. Nadine could waste her time chasing down that story, but she had work to do. She'd spoken to Doe who had lined up movers for Friday morning. The two women had agreed on a one o'clock memorial service for George and Hazel, after which Doe had a meeting with Stan Pemberly to assess damage to the house and sign some necessary business papers. Doe made it clear she had no intention of paying another month's rent on the empty bungalow if she could help it.

True to his word, Joey had removed and disposed of the mattress from the house. Beryl didn't ask how or where. The bedroom window had also been replaced, and the ability to air the room made a big difference to the work environment.

Wednesday evening, six days after the incident at the theater, Beryl stood in the Bennets' laundry room looking into the secret space that contained the safe. She didn't hear Nadine enter the room until her friend spoke, and it was as if she were reading Beryl's thoughts.

"What numbers would you choose if it were your safe?" Nadine asked from the open doorway.

Startled, Beryl spun to face her friend. By the time her heartrate returned to normal, she was able to declare, "Michael's birthday," without hesitation.

"Not your anniversary?" Nadine asked, a wan smile lifting the sides of her mouth.

Beryl shook her head. "No, I don't think so. The first date that popped into my head was the month and day Michael was born, so that would have to be it. What numbers would you pick?" When Nadine hesitated, Beryl teased, "Let me guess … your childhood phone number."

Nadine chuckled. "My first thought was Roger's and my wedding date, but I think I'd choose our son's birthdate instead."

Beryl considered that response for a few seconds, then nodded. "Makes sense." Then she laughed. "Both our safes would be cracked in a New York minute."

"You know," Nadine said, sobering up, "tomorrow would have been the Bennets' fiftieth wedding anniversary. Do you suppose George set those numbers for this combination?"

"Nine, thirty, sixty?" Beryl contemplated, then

corrected herself. "Nine, three, zero, six?" Again, she paused, then shook her head. "Men aren't typically that sentimental. I'm guessing he'd use his social security number or his car's vehicle registration."

"Hazel might have had some input. Surely, she'd need to know and be able to remember the combination," Nadine guessed.

"Well, it's a moot point anyway," Beryl replied with a sigh. She couldn't stop wondering if the contents held secrets of the Bennets' past or clues to their deaths. She closed the lid on the box and turned to Nadine. "I'm not about to break the law by opening this safe. Hopefully, Doe will know the combination, and maybe she'll let us know what's inside."

With those words, Beryl took her friend's arm and gently pulled her toward the door and out to the living room, shutting off the light as they left. The sun had disappeared an hour before the women had gone through the house for the last time, making certain all drawers, cupboards and closets were empty. Cardboard boxes had been carefully labeled and were stacked in each room.

"When are Doe and Kelsey getting here tomorrow?"

"Driving from Grand Junction?" Beryl looked out into the night as she considered the question. "Doe promised they'd be at Sunnydale by one, in time for the service. Afterwards, Stan will accompany her back here to the house to go through the place to settle up any last-minute business. She said she's bringing stickers to mark items for the movers. Joey will meet the truck Friday morning and hang around to close up when they're done."

When the two women reached the patio doors, Beryl turned off the remaining lights as Nadine slid the glass panel aside and stepped outside. Joey had retrieved Beryl's flashlight from the crawl space earlier that afternoon. She picked it up off a carton near the door and removed the makeshift laser-beam cardboard before switching on the light to guide their way across the yard to her house. She gave a last look around and, heaving another sigh, she followed Nadine into the night.

Entering her own living room, Beryl didn't bother turning on lights, but headed straight for the darkened kitchen. Her flashlight caught Smudge on the kitchen counter, eyes glowing bright yellow out of the dark.

"What are you doing up there?" Beryl scolded, rounding the corner. The beam from her torch bounced off a red-and-gold candy wrapper on the floor. "You've been swatting papers again, you naughty cat." She attempted to swipe his back haunches as he disappeared off the edge and raced toward the bedroom. She imagined she could hear him chuckling over his prank.

Beryl rested the bright halogen light on the chair seat she used to balance herself when she leaned over to pick up the foil. As she straightened, she noticed a small hole in the shadow cast by the wrapper onto the wall beneath the countertop. She froze for a second, studying the image. Half bent, she moved the paper slowly back and forth in front of the beam.

"Nadine," she called without taking her eyes from the wall. "Come look at this."

"What are you playing with?" Nadine leaned over to see beyond Beryl's shoulder. "What is that?"

"It's a hole," Beryl replied unnecessarily. Standing upright, she switched on the kitchen overheads. Her actions were slow and methodical while her mind was spinning.

"Smudge has torn it," Nadine said as if the reason for the tear were obvious.

"No, it's not something Smudge would have done. It's too small and precise." Beryl's thoughts weren't completely on what she was saying.

She suddenly swung around, went through the living room and into the bedroom where she'd left the copies of the coat's contents next to her printer. Hurrying back to the pass-through, she spread the sheets out onto the counter, found the one she wanted and reached for her reading glasses. Slipping them onto her nose, she then studied the paper for nearly half a minute. Finally, she slid it across the counter to Nadine.

"See that?" Beryl demanded.

Nadine frowned, puzzled by her friend's excitement. "I see that you made copies of the papers that were in that coat of Kelsey's."

"Look close at the candy wrappers," Beryl ordered.

Take a close look, Nadine mentally modified, but kept silent and did as she was told. It took her nearly half a minute as she examined the images, bringing them in inch or two from her face, then away. She did this a few times before her eyes suddenly widened and she stared over at Beryl. "It looks like the exact same tiny hole in each of the foils. What does it mean?"

"It means," said Beryl, "that I think we just discovered how the blood pressure medicine was administered to Hazel … and probably to George."

Chapter 24

At 12:50 the following afternoon, Beryl was standing outside the dining room at the Big House, surveying the crowd milling around the courtyard. She hadn't been able to reach Butch since her discovery the previous evening and hoped to have a word with him before the service. Nervous and anxious to get through the next hour or so, she glanced over at Nadine and Jessica who were assisting a woman with a walker at the far end of the patio. Henry, Clara and the "ladies in waiting" grouped near them.

More Sunnydale residents filled nearly half of the six rows of folding chairs, their backs to Beryl and the main building. At the foot of the courtyard stood a table draped in a dazzling white cloth. The silver frame holding the photo of George and Hazel Bennet rested in front of a standing wreath of white roses, carnations and lilies. A glass vase overflowing with colorful blossoms adorned each end of the table. The attendees who weren't already seated were admiring the memorial display and talking in low murmurers. One couple seemed to be having a serious conversation with Stan Pemberly who was stationed at the near end of the adorned table.

The lush green lawn, freshly manicured, stretched

out beyond the table and reached toward the foothills of the Rocky Mountains. On this near-perfect day in late September, the slopes were at their loveliest beneath the few puffs of white clouds that floated lazily across a sky as blue as cornflowers.

Looking surreptitiously at her watch for the tenth time in the last two minutes, Beryl hoped again that Butch would arrive before Doe and Kelsey. He'd been out of touch for the past few days, sitting with his wife, daughter and granddaughter at the hospital. His great-grandchild's illness had developed into something critical. The doctors were taking tests, but couldn't seem to ease the baby's breathing. She'd been admitted to the hospital where Butch and Cecily had been keeping vigil with the baby's parents and grandparents. Beryl had been kept informed of the infant's condition through the Yancys' youngest daughter, who had also asked that Beryl not disturb the family unless she had an emergency.

Butch had finally surfaced an hour ago, leaving a message with Sunnydale's receptionist to let Beryl know the baby was out of danger and would be going home. Cryptically, he'd alerted Beryl that he had the news she was waiting for and expected to be at the retirement center in time for the service.

Cutting it close, Beryl thought, torn between concern for the Yancy family and stress over the confrontation to come with Doe and Kelsey.

"Hello there, young lady," Butch's voice came from behind her as he pushed through the glass door and gave her a one-arm hug. Relief flooded through her. Just knowing her friend was near comforted Beryl enough for her to relax a bit. Before she could do more than smile at him, his eyes were straying over the crowd. "Which one is Henry Slater?" he asked, returning his gaze to hers.

Beryl nodded imperceptibly toward the right side of the patio where Nadine stood in quiet conversation with Jessica. "See the woman in the black suit with a royal purple blouse and beret?" she said without looking directly at the group.

"Yup," he answered staring in Clara's direction. "Hard to miss."

Beryl swallowed a laugh and fought to keep her expression neutral, so it took a few seconds for her to speak. "The man she's holding onto for dear life is Henry."

"Gotcha," Butch said, surprising Beryl by removing his arm from her shoulders and heading toward the foursome. Stopping in front of the nattily dressed man, Butch offered his hand as he spoke. After a brief pause during which Henry's expression morphed from surprised to amused, he accepted Butch's hand and replied with a grin.

What does Butch want with Henry? Beryl wondered. She strained to hear what the men were saying, but she was too far away. She noticed, however, that Nadine had turned from Jessica to listen to the conversation, and Clara's eyes were wide as she leaned away to stare up at Henry. Before Beryl could even begin to imagine what Butch was up to, she caught motion out of the corner of her eye. Stan was beckoning her over. Doe Bennet stood at his side and Kelsey Martine slouched behind her mother, arms folded across her chest and a pouty expression on her face.

Beryl had been so engrossed in the interaction between Butch and Henry, she hadn't noticed Doe arrive with her daughter. Switching mental gears and trying to push her friend's peculiar behavior temporarily from her mind, Beryl hurried to greet the newly arrived guests. Almost immediately, Stan asked her to lead the Bennet relatives to reserved seats in the front row, then held up his hands to get everyone's attention. "If you'll please take seats, we'll begin," he announced several times before everyone had heard and obeyed.

Once the crowd settled into quiet expectation, Stan introduced Sunnydale's chaplain and the service began. The pastor was the only speaker. Not surprisingly, Beryl thought, since the Bennets, although friendly enough, hadn't made close friends within the community. Nadine had asked Imogene if she wanted to say a few words, but the woman said she'd prefer to converse with a few select friends at a later date. No mention was made of the last four mysteries Hazel had requested.

Henry, too, had declined to reminisce, Nadine had informed Beryl. Listening to the chaplain, Beryl speculated about Henry's dismissal and wondered how well Henry had actually known the couple. The thought evolved into rabid curiosity. *What on earth was Butch up to?* She didn't want to draw attention to herself by turning to stare, but she was dying to catch her old friend's eye.

The eulogy and prayer ended fairly quickly. Beryl leaned forward in preparation to rise when Kelsey's low demanding voice stopped her.

"Can we go now, Mother," the young woman

muttered between clenched teeth.

"Soon, Kelsey," Doe said in a slightly louder voice. "I do have to thank some people and then we need to go through the house with Stan." She patted her daughter's knee while she reviewed their schedule.

By this time, Beryl was standing. She'd turned her back on the two women, but stayed close enough to eavesdrop on their conversation. She had words for Kelsey, but didn't want to confront the young woman until most, if not all, of the other guests had retreated to the dining room where a buffet of finger sandwiches and cookies had been prepared. On the other hand, she was not about to let the girl escape without answering some very pointed questions.

"I wouldn't have to follow you around like a puppy dog if I'd come in my own car," Kelsey whined.

"The title and insurance haven't been transferred yet, so it's still your grandmother's car," Doe said with a firmness that surprised Beryl. "It would have been silly to drive two cars when you're staying in Grand Junction with me until the estate can be settled. I have to watch our expenses until that's done," Doe went on, sounding like a mother talking to a wayward child. "Now, put that pretty smile back on your face and come speak to the minister with me."

Beryl took that as her cue. Since everyone else had vacated the immediate vicinity, she crossed in front of Doe and stopped before Kelsey. Pulling an object from her pocket, Beryl asked, "Recognize this?" Held between thumb and forefinger was a small plastic bag containing a red-and-gold foil-wrapped candy.

Kelsey looked at the chocolate for several seconds. Her sullen expression didn't change as she raised her eyes to Beryl's without tilting her head. "Yeah, I know what it is. So what?"

"That's one of the candies Hazel was so fond of," Doe spoke up, clearly confused about the confrontation.

"You've been injecting a diuretic into the candy, haven't you?" Beryl's tone made the question more of an accusation as she stared intently at Kelsey.

"Prove it," the young woman retorted, raising one side of her mouth in a half smile, half sneer.

Still holding Kelsey's stare, Beryl put the baggie away and pulled out the sapphire drop earring. "What about this one? Ever seen it before?" she asked with an insincere smile of her own.

For the next few seconds, Kelsey stared blankly at what Beryl had in her palm, but then awareness struck. Kelsey's expression switched from haughty to surprise to shock. "You found that in my coat, didn't you?" she accused.

An idea popped into Beryl's head at that moment. Without thinking, she blurted. "And you came into my home in the middle of the night looking for it." Kelsey said nothing, but Beryl caught the flash of guilt in the young woman's eyes before she turned her head away. "And I'll bet the theater manager will confirm that she told you where to find it," Beryl continued.

Kelsey swept her gaze toward the front of the main building and the parking lot beyond. In the next instant, she spun back and her hand shot out to grab the jewel, but Henry Slater had already moved. As silently as a snake, he had come up behind Beryl and when Kelsey made her move, he struck first and snatched the sapphire from Beryl's hand. Holding the earring up to the sunlight and well out of Kelsey's reach, he studied it briefly.

"I'll have to compare this with the photos on my computer, but I'm sure it was stolen from a widow in Seattle," he said, swiveling to hand the piece to Butch who had moved up to stand behind the small group. "There's a matching necklace and another earring, of course, along with other heirlooms. Perhaps this young lady can help us locate those," Henry added as Butch accepted the sapphire with a simple nod of agreement.

"What is going on here?" Doe demanded. She'd obviously grown impatient over being ignored while others were provoking her daughter, and now her unacknowledged annoyance was boiling into anger.

Without warning, Kelsey turned and began to walk rapidly toward the front of the Big House. Seemingly from nowhere, Jessica appeared from the back row of chairs and strode a few paces alongside the young woman. It looked as if the young firefighter might be escorting Kelsey to the parking lot when, with a wicked smile, Jessica turned and continued to walk in the same direction, only backwards. As she faced Kelsey, still keeping in stride, she threw out an arm like the gate coming down at a railroad crossing.

Furiously, Kelsey pushed at Jessica's forearm. In a flash, Jessica turned the motion and the momentum into an abrupt about-face that resulted in her frog-marching the younger woman back to the gathering.

"What do you think you're doing?" Doe demanded, glaring at Jessica as the mother pulled her daughter into her arms. Holding Kelsey close, Doe glared from Beryl to Henry to Butch and back to Beryl. "Who are these men? I demand you tell me what's going on."

Before Beryl could reply, Joey Marconi rounded the corner of the Big House in the company of two uniformed females. Beryl hadn't remembered seeing Joey before the service and wondered who had alerted him to phone the police. Had Butch set this up? She turned and frowned her silent question at her old friend.

Ignoring her look, the retired detective stepped forward and introduced himself to Doe and Kelsey as Joey and the police neared the group. Butch then tipped his head at Kelsey. "These law officers are here to escort you to the station. You'll need to answer some questions."

"You can't do this," Doe came immediately to her daughter's defense. "My daughter's done nothing wrong."

Beryl wanted to speak her mind on that opinion, but held her tongue. Nadine, who had quietly moved to Beryl's side, patted her friend's wrist in a show of support.

The taller of the two policewomen took hold of Kelsey's arm and tugged gently. "If you'll come with me, please, Miss," she said in a low, stern voice.

"If this is really necessary, I'll drive my daughter to the police station," Doe declared, taking hold of

Kelsey's other arm.

"Fraid you can't do that, ma'am," Butch interrupted, gently removing Doe's hand. Apparently, he relayed a silent message to the officers because the smaller of the two slid between mother and daughter while her partner led Kelsey away. When the second cop headed for the parking lot, Joey took her place.

Probably thinks Doe might try something stupid, Beryl thought in unspoken approval.

"Get out of my way," Doe snarled at Joey as she tugged a mobile phone from her purse. She pushed her way clear, stopping briefly in front of Stan who had been trying to look as small as possible at the end of the white-clothed table. "You'll be hearing from my lawyer," she spat at the Sunnydale manager before stomping off toward the parking lot.

"I need to speak to that woman," Henry said to Butch as he watched Doe's retreating back. "Will you vouch for me at the station?"

"Can't guarantee anything," Butch replied, "but follow me over and I'll see what I can do."

Seeing Butch about to head off, Beryl clutched at his sleeve. "I have a boatload of questions for you."

"Sorry, Beryl. Can't right now. I want to make some introductions." He tipped his chin toward Henry who was heading for his car. "Then, whoever's going to be interviewing Kelsey might want some background from me. I'll call you later," he promised, releasing his arm and walking away.

Stunned by her friend's abrupt dismissal, Beryl looked around at the nearly empty courtyard and up to the glass walls into the crowded dining room. She needed to move out of the hot sun, but she didn't feel like joining the crowd at the buffet. Spinning on her heel, she lowered her head and started for her cottage with long strides.

"Wait." Nadine's voice sounded behind her. "Wait for me," she repeated, catching up with Beryl halfway across the lawn. "I think you should hear this."

"What," Beryl demanded, not slowing her pace.

Nadine followed Beryl to the patio doors and slipped inside before she could shut the glass panel.

Beryl turned, glared and asked again with more than a little impatience, "What is it?"

"Henry," Nadine gasped, trying to catch her breath after running across the lawn. She drew a deep breath and let it out before she was able to continue. "What he said," she sputtered after another long exhale. "You didn't hear."

"Of course I didn't," Beryl answered, trying to control her annoyance. "He was too far away." She wanted desperately to talk to Butch and, during her trip across the lawn, had decided to phone Cecily. Now, first, she had to get rid of Nadine.

"Henry," Nadine breathed raggedly, "is a private investigator."

Chapter 25

"Henry? A private detective?" Beryl said, the incongruous news dropping her into the nearest chair. "You know for sure?"

Nodding, Nadine took a seat on the edge of another nearby chair, her breathing easier by now. "I overheard them. Butch walked up to Henry and said, 'Bernard Yancy, Denver metro area homicide, retired. Friends call me Butch.' That seemed to catch Henry off-guard for a second," Nadine continued to explain, "but when he answered …" She paused to recall the exact words. "He said, 'Henry Slater, Slater Investigations, retired. Friends call me Henry.' Doesn't 'investigations' mean he's a detective?"

"I would say so," Beryl replied. At that moment, she realized what must have happened. She sat straighter in her excitement. "Butch got the results back from the fingerprints on that glass. He's got background on Henry." Her mind whirled as she now wished more than ever to talk to her friend.

"What do you think Henry's doing here at Sunnydale? What would he be investigating? One of us?" Nadine asked, her eyes wide with curiosity.

Beryl thought back to the confrontation in the courtyard. "I don't know, but he told Butch the earring belonged to some woman in Seattle and that there was a necklace to match as well as some other jewelry."

"Wow," Nadine said, slumping back in her chair. "Do you think he's on a case … here at Sunnydale?"

"He did say 'retired,' right?" Beryl asked. She laughed, suddenly drained of energy and tired of speculating. "Maybe we both watch too much TV. Maybe he's here doing what the rest of us are doing … enjoying our golden years."

Nadine looked sheepish. "You're probably right." She squinted at Beryl. "Am I becoming overly suspicious of people?"

"Probably," Beryl said, snickering as she got to her feet. "How about a cup of tea and a sandwich? I never did get to the buffet, did you?"

Nadine shook her head and rose. "Can't, but thanks. I left Imogene in Jessica's care and promised to meet them in the dining room. I know Imogene would like to talk about the service. I suppose she was as close as anyone to Hazel, and she probably needs to reminisce a little."

"Okay," Beryl tried not to show her relief. She had a phone call to make and some time alone would feel good. The afternoon had exhausted her. "Why don't you come by later this evening for a glass of wine. I'd like to rehash today's events, too, but not right now."

Nadine left after agreeing to return at 6:00.

Beryl watched her friend halfway across the lawn before she settled on a kitchen chair and picked up the phone to dial the Yancys' landline. She expected to get their machine, so was startled when Cecily answered.

"What are you doing home?" Beryl blurted.

"Hello to you, too," Butch's wife retorted.

"Sorry," Beryl apologized. "It's just that you surprised me. I thought you might still be with your kids."

"Nope. Just got home. After sitting around the hospital for more hours than I want to count, I badly need a hot shower and a change of clothes." Cecily paused for a second before adding, "What'd you phone for if you didn't expect an answer?"

"I was going to leave a message. I want Butch to call me back as soon as he can," Beryl explained.

"Isn't he with you?" Cecily asked, a hint of alarm in her tone.

"He was," Beryl hurried to assure Cecily, "but he followed our suspect to the station before I could talk to him."

"What is it you'll be wantin'?" Cecily asked. "Maybe I know a thing or two." She chuckled. "It's been known to happen."

Beryl laughed. "How could I forget," she replied before turning serious. "He got the results back from the fingerprints I gave him." Beryl wasn't asking for confirmation, so she didn't wait for an answer. "Do those prints belong to a private detective?"

"You want to know about Henry Slater?" Cecily said with a snort. "That's the name you didn't want to mention the other day, isn't it?"

"Yes," Beryl said. "But now that you know his name, tell me what you found out. Give," she prompted her best friend.

"You're right. Henry Slater is a private investigator from Chicago. Butch told me the guy runs a company that specializes in locating stolen art treasures and other valuables like jewelry and silver. Insurance companies hire him when their wealthy clients get burgled. Is that all you want?" Cecily finished, "because I really do need to get in that shower."

"Okay. Sorry. I'll let you go, but I still want to talk to Butch. I'm pretty sure I know how our suspect murdered Hazel Bennet, and I have some evidence I think will prove it."

"You're not going to share with me, after I spilled my guts just now?" Cecily said, sounding slightly indignant, but amused.

"It's hard to explain unless I can show you," Beryl said. "I've already kept you long enough, so go take your shower," she added, wanting to distract rather than disappoint Cecily. "I'll fill you in later. Just tell Butch to call me, will you?"

Chapter 26

Several hours passed before Beryl got the chance to speak to Butch. Nadine arrived for her glass of wine and brought Jessica with her. The women had barely greeted each other when Joey rapped on the glass.

"Mind if I crash your party," he asked with a hangdog grin when Beryl slid the door open. "Butch didn't have time to fill me in. Said I should talk to you about what happened at the service."

She frowned at the young man, pretending to consider. "I don't have any beer. You'll have to drink wine," she said in a dubious tone.

Playing along, Joey dropped his head as his shoulders slumped. Then, quickly, before Beryl could shut the door on him, he ducked beneath her arm and into the living room.

Laughing, she closed the panel against what was fast becoming a cold night. When she turned to her guests in time to catch a fleeting expression on Joey's face as he greeted Jessica, Beryl wondered if the future policeman might have had a second reason for wanting to join their little soiree. She smiled inwardly as she went through to the kitchen where Nadine was arranging cheese and crackers on a platter.

The group made themselves comfortable in Beryl's living room, wine in hand. She no sooner sat in her favorite chair than Smudge appeared from nowhere and jumped into her lap. With a laugh, she got him settled and was about to pick up her wine glass from the side table when the doorbell rang. With a who-could-that-be frown, she rose, dumping the cat to the floor, and found Butch on the threshold. She pulled him inside, not hiding her pleasure as she gave him a warm hug.

"I thought you'd phone," she said, "but this is much better." She motioned him to join the others while she went to the kitchen for another glass and a second bottle of gewürztraminer. The necessary introduction had been made before she returned to her seat, Jessica being the only one who hadn't yet met Butch Yancy. Small talk continued for several minutes as Beryl again sat down and welcomed Smudge into her lap. Once settled, her curiosity got the better of her hostess manners and she jumped into the conversation, sliding her eyes toward Butch before facing Joey.

"Did you know Henry Slater was a private detective?" she demanded of the man's personal trainer.

"He's a what?" Joey's head snapped away from his conversation with Jessica. "A detective?" he repeated, clearly bewildered. "You kidding me?"

"Retired," Butch said, glancing from Beryl to Joey and back. "Cecily told me you phoned."

Beryl gave him a Cheshire Cat grin, acknowledging his silent accusation of the conspiracy between his wife and herself. She then said seriously, "Henry recognized the sapphire earring, didn't he?" Since the question was rhetorical, she offered a guess. "Part of some loot connected with a case he was working on?"

"Correct on all counts," Butch nodded as he bent forward to put his empty wine glass on the coffee table. Sitting back in the corner of the sofa he shared with Nadine, he draped an arm across the back and glanced around the room. All eyes were on him.

"Is Kelsey Martine a jewel thief as well as a coat thief?" Beryl asked. *Not to mention a murderer*, she thought but didn't say aloud. *One thing at a time.*

Butch gave a short laugh that held no humor. "Yes, she did steal jewelry, but she stole from Hazel who stole from other people first." The room fell silent as the old detective told the story of how Henry Slater had been tracking the couple they knew as George and Hazel Bennet for many years. Their career began in Chicago before they even married. Their son was five when they began to use him in their nefarious schemes. Steven slipped up on one of his first jobs which is when the family came to Henry's attention. Before Slater Investigations had proof enough to confront the Bennets, they disappeared. Henry now knows they changed their names and moved to Seattle where Steven grew up. After their near-arrest in Chicago, George and Hazel learned to be more careful. Doe filled us in on some of this history," Butch explained.

"What a terrible life for a child," murmured Nadine.

"Exactly," Butch agreed. "Fortunately, Steven thought so, too. That's why, at the age of eighteen, after finishing high school, he joined the navy. Left his parents on the west coast and took to sea. When he retired from the service, he settled in Colorado, thinking it was close enough to visit his parents but far enough that they wouldn't recruit him back into the family business."

"If Henry knew who the Bennets were, why didn't he have them arrested?" Nadine asked when Butch stopped to accept a refilled glass from Beryl.

"Not that simple," the old detective replied, sitting back to answer Nadine. "First of all, Henry lost track of them. He was fairly certain they hadn't just gone underground in Chicago, but he didn't know where they were living until a few years ago. Purely by accident, he heard about a couple who had scammed a wealthy widow in Seattle and gotten away with slightly more than a million dollars in jewelry. Henry recognized the M.O. and realized he'd picked up the trail of the pair that had eluded him for most of his career. It took him another year, but he finally tracked them here to Sunnyvale. He was ninety-nine percent certain he'd found his culprits, but lacked the proof to have them charged with anything."

"That's why he wanted me to look through their house," Joey blurted with sudden realization as to his mission in the Bennets' home.

"Most likely," Butch nodded. "Makes sense to have someone look around who might have a legitimate reason for being in the house.

"And now the earring provides the proof Henry's been looking for," Beryl observed. With a touch of black humor, she added, "Just a little late, isn't it?"

"Wait," Jessica interrupted, "if Doe knew about

the Bennets' criminal activities, why didn't she notify the police? If she knew and protected them, doesn't that make her an accessory after the fact?"

Butch shrugged. "She claims not to have known until after George's funeral. Hazel's pain got very bad that night. She had a high fever and Doe was about to call the emergency line when her mother-in-law started to babble, apparently talking to her husband about some jewelry in a safe."

"That must be why Doe stayed in the room whenever anyone visited Hazel," Beryl said, almost to herself. She looked at Nadine, voicing the answer to another question they'd asked each other. "It also explains why she kept Hazel at home and never asked for help, other than from Kelsey." She turned back to Butch. "So Doe learned about the jewelry. What about Hazel's death? We know she was drugged and we're pretty sure Kelsey is guilty, but do you think Doe was also in on it?"

Butch shook his head. "At this point, my gut tells me she's innocent, but they're still questioning her. She hasn't been allowed to speak to her daughter yet, but she's been cooperative with the detectives, so far."

"Does Butch know what you discovered last night?" Nadine asked.

Up to that moment, Beryl had been so absorbed in hearing about Henry that she hadn't wanted to interrupt. Now, she rose, dumping a reluctant Smudge onto the floor for the second time, and went into her bedroom to fetch the folder holding the papers from the coat and the photocopies she'd made. Returning to the living room, she handed

Butch the copies and pointed out the similar pinpricks in each of the foil wrappers.

Nadine asked for one of the copies that she then handed to Jessica. "This is what I was telling you about."

Jessica shared the page with Joey while Beryl explained how she had discovered the holes and what she and Nadine had concluded. "I have the piece of candy Nadine found under Hazel's mattress," Beryl informed Butch. "I think Kelsey may have destroyed any others, so I'm hoping this one will contain hydro-whatsis ..." She frowned at Nadine.

"Hydrochlorothiazide," she helped.

"Right." Beryl turned back to Butch. "That'll prove how Hazel was drugged, so all you need is Kelsey's confession."

Butch snorted a laugh. "Easy for you to say," he quipped.

"George was insulin-dependent, so there would have been syringes in the house," Nadine offered. "We didn't find any when we packed up the place, but maybe Kelsey has some in her luggage or at their home in Grand Junction. She could dose the candy for Hazel. If Kelsey caused George's death, too, she probably added the hydrochlorothiazide to his insulin, since he wouldn't have been eating many chocolate-covered cherries."

Butch raised an eyebrow in thought. After a brief pause, he stood. "I'll call and let them know what you've just told me."

Beryl escorted him to the kitchen where she handed him the baggie containing the chocolate-covered cherry. Storing it in a jacket pocket, he then stepped outside to phone the police station. Five minutes later, Beryl was about to go see what was keeping him, when the detective returned. This time, sensing his fate, Smudge jumped out of her her lap and disappeared into the bedroom.

"They're working on a search warrant," Butch informed the group as he sat back on his end of the sofa. "On a different subject, Kelsey's admitted to starting the fire. She's been searching the house whenever she's felt she wouldn't be seen. That morning, just before dawn, she was on Hazel's bed, going through some papers she'd found in one of the bureau drawers. She was using a candle for light and dropped it when she heard what she thought was someone trying to break in through the bedroom window. The little idiot just dropped the candle and ran out of the house."

"She wasn't very careful with her candle, either," Jessica interjected. "Quite a lot of wax had dripped onto the papers and bedspread, and that accelerated the fire. The smoldering bedspread was what created so much smoke."

Butch shook his head at the stupidity and carelessness before he continued, "Henry's still at the station, so when he heard what Kelsey admitted, he guessed that he was probably that 'someone.' Said he'd been out for an early morning walk when he thought he saw a flickering light in the house. He went up to the window to get a better look. It's a high window, as you know, so he had to pull himself up by the edge of the sill to see anything. The noise she heard must have been his boots scrabbling against the siding."

"What about Doe? Is any of this news to her or has she been in on it from the beginning?" Beryl wanted to know.

"Apparently, Kelsey has cleared her mother of any wrongdoing. She's admitted to taking her step-father's medication without Doe's knowledge, but keeps insisting she didn't have a particular reason for taking it. She's also sticking to her story that Hazel gave her the jewelry. She knows there's more jewelry somewhere in the house, but she doesn't know where. Claims if it's found, Hazel promised it to her."

"The laundry room safe," Beryl and Joey said in unison, looking at each other with instant knowledge. Beryl then explained to Butch about the safe hidden beneath the box beneath Smudge's dishes.

"Have you opened it?" Butch asked.

"That would be illegal," Beryl replied with a twinkle in her eye. When Butch narrowed his eyes at her, she said hastily, "No. Seriously, I know enough not to have touched it."

"We think we know the combination, though," Nadine said, glancing at Beryl before turning to Butch. "At least I'm fairly certain that's what FRAME means on the back of the library receipt. It has to do with their anniversary date on the bottom of that silver frame that holds their photograph." She looked again at Beryl. "It finally makes sense and it's the only explanation."

Butch leaned forward as if ready to rise. "Whatever jewelry is found will be examined by Henry Slater first. As for Kelsey, it looks like greed got the better of her. The money Doe inherited from

Steven had already been spent, and, since it hadn't paid off in an acting career, Doe was insisting that Kelsey look for a paying job. Guess Kelsey preferred to inherit money rather than earn it." With those words, Butch stood, pulling the baggie from his pocket. "I need to drop this off at the station and get on home. Cecily will be wondering what's become of me," he said with a wave to everyone and a hug for Beryl.

After the front door closed behind the old detective, Joey spoke up. "Jessica and I want to go somewhere for pizza. How about you?"

Beryl looked at Nadine who, with her back to the youngsters, winked and gave an imperceptible shake of her head. Beryl silently agreed that she didn't want to intrude on a newly budding friendship. When she said, "Thanks, but you two go along," neither Joey nor Jessica protested, but said "Good night" and slipped out the patio door.

Beryl settled herself in the corner of the couch where Butch had been sitting, shifting to look at Nadine. "I'm so keyed up, I think I need to do something, but don't know what."

A twinkle came into Nadine's eye a second before she said, "I think I'm getting the hang of this detecting business. Do you suppose we could …"

Beryl grabbed a nearby sofa pillow and hurled it at her friend before Nadine could finish the thought.

# # #

Acknowledgments

For this story, I am particularly indebted to three talented and knowledgeable women. Thank you, Angela Marriott, for sharing your firefighter's experience. Thank you, Jan Robinson, for your expertise in the workings of each and every muscle in our bodies. Thank you, Jay Neal, for your insights into community life.

As always, my first readers have been incredibly generous with their time, skill and input on all aspects of pre-publishing this book. Thank you, Sally Hobler, Gail Lindsey and Jan Reynolds!

I don't know what I'd do without Karen Phillips, the artist who has designed all but two of my book covers. She has an amazing talent for conjuring up the perfect picture to illustrate my story.

Once again, I owe a great deal to my critique partner Bonnie McCune (BonnieMcCune.com) who has worked with me since 2000. Her wonderful literary knowledge, comments and suggestions are invaluable.

Last but certainly not least, my deepest gratitude goes to my family, friends and readers who have been so supportive and encouraging. You make my efforts truly rewarding.

About the Author

Suzanne Young was born and raised in Rhode Island. She has worked as a photographer, a writer, an editor, and a computer programmer and business analyst since earning her degree in English from the University of Rhode Island.

A resident of Colorado for nearly 50 years, she retired from software development in 2010 to write fiction full time.

She is a member of Denver Woman's Press Club, Rocky Mountain Fiction Writers and Sisters in Crime as well as a graduate of the Arvada (CO) Citizens Police Academy and a member of Clear Creek Optimists.

To learn more about this author, she invites you to visit her website at http://SuzanneYoungBooks.com. You can also contact her via e-mail at Suzanne@SuzanneYoungBooks.com.